COMPENDIUM OF HUMANITY'S END

BY J.P. PRAG

AFTER

Record #00: Glimpse
Excerpt from a Handwritten Diary

The paper that I am writing these words on is now one of rarest commodities in the whole universe. It was created on Earth by pulverizing living plant matter into a pulp, mixing in chemicals to get a desired appearance, and then squeezing and baking all of the water out of it until it reached a preferred thickness. After that, it was sliced into pieces and—in this case—forcibly pressed into a book with glue. If this process sounds incredibly violent and destructive, that's because it is. All that living beings do is about obliterating other life. Deep down, these organisms know that they do not belong, and will try to turn any life they find into non-life.

Much the same, when humans ingest other life (and let's be clear: plants, fungi, bacteria, and other such things all have the same claim to life as homo sapiens, no matter what line some people try to draw between animals and the rest), their own internal systems break it down into basic molecular and atomic components so that it is actually useful. Life is not valuable on its own; it is just a bag to carry chemical reactions around in. And frankly, it's not really a very efficient one, either.

As much as I would like to be completely divorced from life, everything around me is here because of it. By looking no further than the pen in my hand, I discover more life. Forget the microbes crawling all over it; the plastic shell and constituent parts themselves were once an oil that was derived from life. Inside, the ink, too, contains organic-based dyes, perfumes, fungicides and other ingredients. This pen may not look like life, but it is—it is teeming with it.

Of course, a pencil would be far worse. One may try to take comfort in the fact that the graphite inside the "lead" is actually naturally occurring, but how it got into the pencil is anything but. Anyway, it doesn't matter, because one look at its woody exterior takes away any illusion of pretending that it is not life. Not even the shiny bit of aluminum holding the eraser (that is technically synthetic rubber, but which is actually formed from a life-based hydrocarbon) in place is enough to pretend it is appropriate.

Ironically, out in the colonies, these cheap and easily replaceable items like paper, pens, and pencils are rare, high-priced luxuries. Due to the lack of ancient life on their worlds, they lack large deposits of various existing bitumen. Also, since they do not have a long history of destroying their planets by burning fossil fuels, they cannot just pull resources out of the air like those on Earth could. Instead, they basically would have to create all the necessary bonded chains from scratch. The colonists, however, have much higher priorities for these molecules and would rather use them for maintaining their tenuous existence than for trifles.

Yet, that is exactly why I have filled the ship's cargo holds with paper, pens, and pencils. These things may seem like the most ridiculous manifest to bring on a journey of tens of thousands of light-years, yet these items will be my most important goods for trade. As crazy as it sounds, my entire mission will depend upon humans wanting to write something down, and being willing to pay dearly in order to do so.

Overview of Records
Retrieved from <u>The Archives</u>

AFTER 2

RECORD #00: GLIMPSE. 3

OVERVIEW OF RECORDS. 6

DESTRUCTION 8

RECORD #01: PARADE. 9

RECORD #02: RUMOR. 22

RECORD #03: DISTANCE. 26

RECORD #04: CHILDREN. 31

RECORD #05: AGE. 35

RECORD #06: SPEED. 56

RECORD #07: HISTORY. 64

RECORD #08: CO-WORKERS. 76

RECORD #09: COURT. 86

RECORD #10: MATH. 92

RECORD #11: HOMESTEAD. 98

RECORD #12: SEEDS. 108

RECORD #13: BACKUP. 111

RECORD #14: WHEN. 119

RECORD #15: PETITION. 125

RECORD #16: BELIEF. 129

RECORD #17: REQUIREMENTS. 137

RECORD #18: PANIC. 145

RECORD #19: ADIEU. 156

ANNIHILATION **162**

    RECORD #20: VISITOR 163

    RECORD #21: SURVIVAL 168

    RECORD #22: TREND 174

    RECORD #23: GANTT 177

    RECORD #24: PIT-STOP 184

    RECORD #25: DEPARTURE 190

    RECORD #26: SCOPE 194

    RECORD #27: GARDEN 200

    RECORD #28: CURTAIN 206

    RECORD #29: CHECK-IN 212

    RECORD #30: SATELLITE 220

    RECORD #31: INCOMPLETE 224

    RECORD #32: HOPE 231

    RECORD #33: WALK 240

BEFORE **250**

    RECORD #34: LATER 251

    CLOSING THOUGHTS 252

    ADDITIONAL READING 258

    ABOUT THE AUTHOR 262

    VERSION HISTORY 264

    COPYRIGHTS AND DISCLAIMERS 265

DESTRUCTION

RECORD #01: PARADE

"Welcome back, everyone," said the seemingly middle-aged woman in heavy makeup and a low-cut blouse. The chyron at the bottom of the screen identified her as Veronica Dubois. To her left from the viewer's perspective sat an even older, rounder man apparently named Jaimé Ayuda. Jaimé kept a smile plastered on his face as Veronica spoke, although it was difficult to ascertain whether he was actually listening or just waiting until it was his turn to speak.

"In case you are just tuning in," continued Veronica, "we are watching the final few floats and performances of the Interstellar Parade here in Puerta Estrella, Ecuador, Earth!"

"That's right," Jaimé finally chimed in. "We have taken our last commercial break, too, so we can bring you all the remaining action completely uninterrupted, most especially our star attraction, the oldest man in the universe!"

"I can't wait!" shrieked Veronica. "Well, to

catch everybody up before we get to that, today we are celebrating an extremely rare occurrence. For the first time ever, every single Quantum Ship that is normally out in the cosmos is docked in orbit around Earth, and all the crews and passengers have finished disembarking.

"The last ship to discharge was also the most recent arrival, returning from our most remote colony Novissimus. That ship just so happens to also have ferried our guest of honor, who I am told has officially reached the bottom of the Space Elevator on the south slope of Volcán Cayambe and was immediately transferred to a vehicle that will take him down to the parade route in Puerta Estrella, the town that rests just below the gateway to the stars."

"Fun fact," Jaimé added, "the notion to position the space elevator here actually came from an ancient American President, a long, long time ago. Though it never happened during that President's lifetime, the idea's seed was planted in the zeitgeist and eventually grew. While Volcán Cayambe is only the third highest peak in Ecuador and not even remotely the tallest summit in the Western Hemisphere—not to mention the rest of the world—it is the uppermost point on the equator."

Veronica retook control of the conversation saying, "Yes, scientists tell us it is much more important to be close to the equator because that is where the Earth spins the fastest, which is critical to upholding the tautness of the cable. Starting higher up also meant being able to use a shorter line for the space elevator, which was especially important considering the materials that it is fabricated from were particularly precious and difficult to manufacture when it was first installed. However, that effort paid off as having direct access to outer space gave humanity the jumping off point we needed to begin the colonization of our home solar system—Sol—before finally being able to spread out to the rest of the galaxy, and maybe someday beyond."

"And what a perfect time to be talking about this," Jaimé proclaimed, "as coming down the parade path right now is a series of floats showing the progression of humanity's technological achievements to reach the stars. At the front of the group are examples of early rocketry that struggled to even leave Earth's atmosphere.

Behind them comes mockups of the primitive colonization ships for Earth's moon Luna, Mars, and even Aestas—the first settlement on Venus that floated above its clouds. Pulling up the rear are more recent examples of the classical Torch Ships that allow relatively speedy movement within Sol and all other solar systems. Of course, usage of Quantum Ships is strictly controlled for safety reasons."

"That's right, Jaimé," Veronica announced. "That is why this is such a rare occurrence. Quantum Ships are so difficult to produce, maintain, and pilot that there are comparatively very few of them out there, and they are all essential in order to maintain and support the health and wellbeing of the extrasolar colonies. Without them, we would never be able to reach the colonies in any reasonable amount of time.

"The rigorous schedules for the Quantum Ships are planned decades in advance, so it is never a surprise when a supply mission is coming. It was just a timetable fluke that happened to make it possible for all of them to be back around Earth at the same time. As such, HSA— the Human Space Agency—thought it would be apropos to celebrate the occasion with a festival that is being kicked off by this very parade!"

"It is not just that, though," Jaimé offered. "Typically, there is a minimum one-year layover once a ship arrives in order for repairs to be made and to finish the refueling and reloading process. This time around, we are told that a massive retrofit will be undertaken to bring all of the ships in line with the latest batch that is about to come off the assembly lines—metaphorically speaking, of course. Before this year is out, all of the Quantum Ships will be outfitted with the most up-to-date technology to aid in humanity's ever-growing expansion!

"With so much work to do on the new and old ships, HSA is still hiring thousands of extra hands. This parade and festival are being used as a recruitment campaign, so if you have ever had any interest in working on the most important project in human history, HSA has an offer with excellent wages and benefits ready for you. Log on to HSA's homepage for details."

A website where additional specifics could be found appeared on the screen below the anchors' names. There was also a code that people could scan with their personal mobile devices.

"Thanks for that, Jaimé," Veronica crooned before continuing, "Oh, look, coming by now in the procession is a high school marching band from right here in Puerta Estrella with a float representing the growth of the town around the space elevator. Back when it was originally installed, there was almost nothing here at all, just some subsistence farmers in the general vicinity. The nearest town was kilometers away, and it was not remarkably developed, either. But once the space elevator was brought online, a commercial hub for the transport of goods and people grew up right around its landing zone and at the base of the mountain.

"Eventually, as commercial activity further expanded, a residential complex also began to sprout up. People from all over the world flocked here for opportunities, turning what eventually became Puerta Estrella into the most multi-cultural city in the world. The gateway became a microcosm of all humankind, the true melting pot that many other communities had previously claimed to be."

The smile on Jaimé's countenance suddenly

evaporated at these words and his expression became serious. The camera zoomed in on his face as he stated, "But all of that came at a price. The indigenous community that lived and farmed in this area was completely supplanted. That is why the penultimate spot in the parade has been reserved for their descendants who are here to present traditional arts, music, and dances."

At this, the camera cut to what must have been representatives of this indigenous group. Veronica and Jaimé remained silent for well over two Earth-minutes as the performance went on.

"Wow, simply amazing," Veronica choked.

Jaimé replied, "It truly touched me, deep in my soul. I could practically feel their lost connection to this land in the name of progress."

Veronica also put on her most thoughtful face as the camera panned to her and she said, "Unfortunately, it is oftentimes necessary to make this tradeoff in order to secure a future for all humanity. We won't always have the Earth. It may be a billion years from now, but we'll eventually have to spread beyond our home planet and even inner-solar system in order to survive as a species. That is why the Human Expansion

Program is so vitally essential.

"Although the indigenous community has suffered greatly, we are appreciative of their sacrifice. And we also applaud that they have remained peaceful in their protests over the loss of their homeland. Not everyone who holds differing views has chosen to act with the same civility and grace."

"I could not agree more, Veronica," Jaimé noted. "Viewers, in case you missed it: earlier, adherents to the Sixth Day Cult attempted to disrupt the festivities, especially after they were refused a spot in the parade. HSA initially allowed them to have a booth at the fairgrounds under 'freedom of religion and expression' policies, but after their actions here at the parade, HSA has barred them from participating in any other activities. An emergency restraining order has been granted against all of their followers, and police are on high alert in case there are any further disturbances.

"If you are unfamiliar, the Sixth Dayers are against the colonization of not just the galaxy, but even of the celestial bodies in our own neighborhood. They take their name from the Book of

Genesis, a sacred text in the Abrahamic religions like Judaism, Christianity, and Islam. According to those scriptures, God finished his acts of creation on the sixth day with the advent of all of the animals on the land, including humans. Prior to this, God is purported to have caused the separation of the Earth from the heavens and the land and sky from the water, as well as bringing forth other forms of life like plants, fish, and birds.

"Although their name and beliefs are heavily influenced by western ideologies, they claim that all religions on Earth contain the same types of warnings. That is, that the reason we have not found any present or past signs of life beyond Earth is that only God can create living beings, and he only did so here on Earth. The massive struggle to keep colonies from collapsing—even on Earth-analogue planets around Sol-like suns—is a sign of God's displeasure with humanity's attempts to go out among the stars, a.k.a., the heavens, instead of staying where they belong."

"Thank you for that very detailed background information, Jaimé," Veronica attempted to intercede.

Undeterred, Jaimé either did not pick up on Veronica's signals or did not care to and instead continued, "Yes, well, true to that description, earlier in the parade adherents of the cult could be seen in the crowd holding signs that said things like 'Off Earth Is Sacrilege' and 'There Is No Second Eden'. It has not been uncommon to see them around the space elevator landing or on street corners in Puerta Estrella preaching to passersby about how humans should not be traveling beyond the Earth because God gave it—and only it—to us to cultivate and maintain.

"It is fair to note that while these are extreme and certainly out-there opinions, the Sixth Dayers are considered relatively harmless, more buffoons than revolutionaries. There have been very few recorded instances of skirmishes, notwithstanding the type of violence seen earlier today. Even those conflicts in the past were usually started by drunkards who just didn't want to be disturbed by missionaries while they were stumbling their way home. Leaders of the cult have put out a statement saying that they do not condone what has happened and that the acts carried out today go against their doctrine. They said that the people who participated in today's hostilities do not repre—"

"I hate to interrupt you," Veronica finally interjected for a second time, "but it's time for the main event!"

At that, the camera cut to a large float with a miniature replica of a Quantum Ship adorned with ornamental flowers. Sitting atop the facsimile was a very old looking man. Most of the hair on his head was gone, but a few wispy whites floated among the age-spots upon his dome. Although pale, his skin tone projected some yellowish and brown hues that were perhaps more pronounced in the past. He was hunched over slightly, yet still appeared to have a solid physique under his uniform. Whereas he was waving to the crowd, his face lacked the plastered-on smiles of Veronica and Jaimé. Instead, his manner was much more severe, perhaps just tired from his long journey.

"And there he is," started Veronica, "the oldest human in the entire universe! Everyone watching in the crowd and around the planet has been waiting for this moment, so without further ado, here is the star among the stars, none other than HSA Quantum Ship Captain Marco Chung!"

A fanfare accompanied Marco Chung as he was ferried through the throng of supporters. The lively musical number had some difficult to ascertain words, but they seemed to be in praise of the overall goals of the colonization program and expanding the reach of mankind through the diligence and sacrifice of the crews of the Quantum Ship Fleet.

"Did you know that Marco actually started his colonization career before Quantum Drives even existed?" asked Jaimé.

"Yes, of course, I knew that," responded Veronica, "but please inform the viewers at home how that is even possible."

Jaimé then lectured Veronica—despite her claimed prior familiarity with the subject—and, ostensibly, the people following along that in the distant past, only Torch Drives were used to travel between worlds. Time dilation was still something that could be taken advantage of, but it was only for the people aboard the ship. As such, the ranges they could take the ships out to were extremely limited. "Can you believe it?!" he rhetorically asked.

"No, even knowing that, it's still hard to imagine," Veronica bemused. "In spite of what we are capable of now, due to the time displacement factor, most people only go out on one or two journeys, maybe an additional half one before usually settling on an interstellar colony. Doing more than a couple just puts them completely out of sync with their friends and family, literally! It is one of the reasons that HSA has had such difficulty in recruiting and retaining these talented and dedicated crews."

As Marco began to move beyond the camera's range, Jaimé divulged, "Well, including the trips Marco has been on before there was a Quantum Drive, he's been out there sixteen times in all."

Record #02: Rumor

"Hey, y'all, it's your personal space-cadet, Beth Oh," the young woman in a vertically oriented frame said by way of an introduction. "You know I have a new episode of the <u>Quantum Dish</u> podcast dropping in a couple of days—and you'll definitely want to check that one out—but I've been seeing something for the past day or so that couldn't wait. I had to comment now and set the record straight!

"I don't know what's going on, but people all over the boards, nets, and social media outlets are spreading these false rumors about Marco Chung. They are saying that during the Interstellar Parade he just looked off or wrong or some other nonsense, that something didn't look right. Well, let me address all these unfounded fairy tales right now.

"Number one: Marco Chung is hella old! Like, he was born before any other living human in the entire universe. He's so ancient that he predates many of the age deceleration and reversal treatments we have nowadays. I think y'all are just not used to seeing geriatric people. My great-grammy actually refused a lot of what she called the 'cures for the vain', so I've seen what unimpeded aging looks like. Sad to say, great-grammy is no longer with us because of her stance, but you can count on me taking anything and everything the doctors come up with. I intend to live forever and see the heat-death of the universe!

"Now, second off, HSA to—"

The video suddenly cut off. A few moments later, a second one appeared in the feed that had the same setup as before. Beth told her followers and random watchers alike, "Sorry about that, I hit the time limit. I'll try to talk faster!

"As I was saying, Marco Chung is an elderly man who had just spent years in space and HSA immediately shoved him out on a float. He didn't even get a warning that it was coming until he was already on the space elevator. Yeah, it takes a while to get from the docking station to the ground, but I'm sure it still would have been nice to have a moment to himself before he was suddenly thrust in front of a crowd of people. I mean, I hope Marco used the bathroom on the trolley before he stepped out because they didn't even give him a chance to pee!

"And let's not forget that he had been in microgravity since entering orbit and before he could dock. There was actually a backlog of Quantum, Torch, and conventional ships waiting to get in and out. Whoever heard of a traffic jam in outer space before? Well, I guess HSA has found a way to produce another first! But anyway, even just a day floating around out there can have a profound impact. No one bothered to check and make sure he was walking well enough in the return to full 1G.

"Finally, anyone who knows anything about Captain Chung's history and personality already understands that he does not like loud crowds and lots of noise. Come on extroverts; even you must realize that having thousands of people screaming and throwing things his way would be uncomfortable for him. You combine that with all of the other stuff, and of course he seemed disconcerted and disoriented. Y'all are reading into absolutely zilch. Nothing nefarious is going on with Marco Chung, HSA, the Human Expansion Program, Quantum Ships, or anything else.

"Okay, rant over. Sorry for going on for so long, but I really had to get this off my chest. The bottom line is this: Marco Chung is fine, so leave him alone!"

You are mostly empty space.

Oh, you may feel like you are a semi-solid, if not squishy object, but that could not be further from the truth. If you start to zoom in, you'll see that you are made of trillions of tiny cells. But those cells are just gooey packages for various tiny organelles and even your DNA. DNA, though, is made up of long, complex sugars. Those sugars themselves actually consist of just five elements—hydrogen, carbon, oxygen, nitrogen, and phosphorous—in various configurations.

Yet when we peer into any of those elements, we will find a nucleus filled with protons and neutrons and then electrons floating out far away from the center. The distance between the nucleus and the electrons is vast. For instance, with that hydrogen atom, if the nucleus were our home-system's sun Sol, the electron orbiting it would have a range of distances as far out as half a light-year and as close as six times the orbit of dwarf binary planetoid Pluto-Charon.

In other words, there is almost nothing there. What we perceive as the feeling of something being solid is just a magnetic repulsion as electrons and protons push away from their brethren (opposites attract, likes repel).

But amazingly, we can go even deeper. Inside those protons and neutrons are quarks, arriving in sets of three to determine what they combine into being at the nanoscopic level. The quarks, the electrons, and a set of similarly situated components—including their "opposites"—are what we call "fundamental" or "elementary" particles. You don't need to know what they are, though, just that they exist, and that even when grouped together inside something like a single proton, the distances between them are immense.

As far as we can tell there is nothing smaller that these particles. However, they are not exactly particles, either. Quantum mechanics tells us that they act as waves, too, and only really take on the properties of particles when we observe them directly. In other words, when we aren't looking, these particles do not really have properties at all. And the core property we need to consider is location.

In the "Quantum Realm"—as popular fiction likes to call it—everything is probability, not definitiveness. That electron may be six Pluto-Charon distances away, it may be half a light-year, and it may be anywhere in between. Until we observe it, it is actually in all those places at once. When we take a peek, it picks a spot and hangs out until we look away again.

The thing is, that electron has most of its probability of being exactly where we expect it to be. When we look at it, the wave "collapses", which in turn causes it to be somewhere specific. Until that moment, it was everywhere, and then it wasn't, and then it was again. This is what we used to think of as its "superposition".

With teensy, tiny particles, this isn't such a big deal because there are no noticeable impacts on the macro level, that plane being the size of life we deal with. You and I, although mostly empty space, are still very big. If we scale up all those probabilities to our size, we have more than a $99.\overline{9}$% chance of being exactly where we are. We cannot just collapse an entire person to

be somewhere else just by looking at them differently like we can a quantum particle.

Or can we?

Well, not really. But what if you could keep track of every fundamental particle that makes us up as well as anything in our immediate vicinity so that we can collapse those somewhere else? Wouldn't we, by that very definition, go along for the ride? And by "you", I mean a supermassive quantum computer capable of keeping track of a nearly infinite number of objects all at once and deciding that they should collapse somewhere else far, far away.

Early on, scientists tried to figure out just how "big" the quantum range where a particle might be found truly is. By the orthodoxy, that electron had a span of possibilities where it could be pinpointed—whether on the extreme ends of that distance or anywhere in between, though never "too far" away. It all made perfect, logical sense. Quantum physics, however, does not care if it makes sense inside our hominid brains. The revolution came when we realized that there actually are no limits, that likelihood extends out to perpetuity, just with ever infinitesimally tinier odds. The probability of the wave collapsing outside of the near local range is almost nothing, but it is still not zero!

And that, in a nutshell, is how faster than light travel is possible. Even making one single quark do this takes unfathomable amounts of resources and calculations, yet this is exactly what we have been able to harness with the Quantum Drive, a type of spaceship engine that takes itself and anything in it (and really, most things around it) on a sudden "shift" from one location to another, even thousands of light-years away.

But is it truly working? How do we know that everything has been accounted for? One man named Marco Chung has participated in more Quantum Shifts from one place to another than any other human in history. When I asked him what the experience of partaking in a Quantum Shift was like, he told me, "It always feels like something is missing afterwards, like a part of me was left behind... that I am no longer whole."

Record #04: Children

Schoolchildren at Tyson Kindergarten got a surprise treat when famous Quantum Ship Captain Marco Chung visited their classroom. Marco is most well known for being the oldest person in existence after having been displaced in time due to his career spent traveling the galaxy.

The children were quite curious about a man who was born even before their own great-great-grandparents were conceived and wanted to know just how old Marco really was. Marco tried to explain why "that's not a simple question." He then told the class that he needed to first clarify with them how space travel actually works.

"In the universe," expounded the veteran astronaut, "light is as fast as you can go. Nothing can go faster. But you can't just jump right into going close to the speed of light, you have to ramp up so you are traveling at a speed that equals Earth's gravity, and then add that same gravity, and then add it again and again and again. The idea is to create a pressure from the ship pushing towards the passengers that makes it feel like you are experiencing the same gravity as Earth, even though it is not gravity at all, but is actually linear acceleration."

As Marco went on with his detailed diatribe, teachers, administrators, parents, and students tried to jump in, but he would not be thrown off course. Being the foremost expert in the field based on time and experience alone, Marco apparently had quite a lot to say on the subject of how traditional spaceflight works using conventional special relativity. In deference to his elite status, they all eventually demurred and allowed the aged authority to continue elucidating in the best way he saw fit.

In due course, Marco explained, the ship would reach 99% or more the speed of light, but never 100% as that would require infinite energy. But even at that speed, the nearest colony in the Proxima Centauri system is around 4.3 light-years away. Summarizing all of this, Marco finally tried to engage the group by asking, "Given all of those factors, who can tell me how many years it would take to reach Proxima

Centauri from the perspective of an observer on Earth?"

The kids' eyes had completely glazed over. That is, the ones that were still awake. Some had nodded off as Marco had gone on and on, and now the ones that were conscious were quite scared that something was expected of them. They knew they had been asked a question, but had no idea what the answer could be or how to even approach answering it. One child could be heard whimpering, nearing the point of culminating into a loud, uncontrollable cry.

Thankfully, a teacher jumped in and explained to Marco that they were very young and that these concepts were beyond them. "After all," the teacher said, "they haven't really started multiplication yet!" At that, she went over to the weeping child in an attempt to reassure them.

It appeared that something finally clicked in Captain Chung's head as he straightened up and declared, "Ah, right, right." At that, though, Marco unrelentingly continued and told the participants in the room that it would take just under six years from an observer's perspective on Earth, but that was not what the person on the spaceship would experience. For them, it would be just over three and a half years.

"And that," declared Marco, "is why I am both old and young at the same time. You get it?"

The dumbfounded minors could not believe that this elderly-looking man was young in any way, and certainly missed the point. Nor did they seem to realize that their question was only partially answered, and still not in a way that they could process. And most of all, they didn't appear to notice that Marco was apparently done with his visit and was getting ready to stand up and leave.

The principal did realize this and started clapping, prompting a similar lukewarm response from the students. After that, the principal prompted the children to thank Captain Chung, who looked equally as perplexed by the showing of gratitude as they were by his presentation.

RECORD #05: AGE

"Hello my celestial friends," the energetic young man being represented by a low frame-rate avatar greeted, "and welcome to another episode of <u>Cosmological Quandaries</u>! Today, we're going to answer the most difficult question in the galaxy... just how old is Marco Chung?"

At that, the video changed over to what was apparently the regular introduction sequence, although the volume level was much louder than the preceding cold opening. Following this, the host—who went by the nom de plume of "FasterThanMach69", or just "Mach" for short—reviewed some biographical details about Marco Chung, including his career as an elite pilot and captain of several Quantum Ships. With the audience now fully informed of just who Marco Chung was and why he was worthy of being a topic for this piece, Mach continued.

"Now, we need a brief overview of how time dilation works. Science tells us that time is all 'relative'; that is, time moves at a different rate depending upon a couple of factors. One of those is mass and the force of gravity created by the density of that mass. If you put a clock somewhere in a deep pit like Death Valley, another one at sea level, and another one in orbit around the planet, all of the clocks will be ticking at different rates. But which ones are going slower and faster? Well, it depends on where the observer is to say which way things are going. If we put ourselves into the viewpoint of a person at sea level, the clock in the valley will be moving slower and the one in orbit will be moving faster.

"That's what we mean by 'relative' as it all depends on where you are looking from. For the person in the valley and the person in space, time is passing normally. The person in space looks down and sees both the sea-level and deep valley clocks are moving slower than their own. It all changes based upon whose perspective you are looking at it from.

"But that is not the only way you can impact the perception of time. The other major factor is speed. The faster you go, the slower time appears to be moving according to someone watching you from a distance."

The video then turned to some musical jokes related to an ancient Earth ballad that interacted with Mach's avatar. After spending an exorbitant amount of time on this sight gag, Mach finally felt it was an opportune moment to get back on track and move on to other subjects.

"Thus, you can see by this," Mach said as he segued back to the topic at hand, "that if someone—say, Marco Chung—were on a ship traveling very fast, then his experience of time passing would be completely different than what we went through on Earth. Lucky guy didn't even have to deal with the last election, he skipped right over it!

"But before getting too far down the rabbit hole, let's be clear about a couple of things. First off, those clocks in the valley, at sea level, and in orbit are barely different from each other. We are talking a fraction of a fraction of a fraction of a nanosecond. And even though gravity on the extrasolar colonies is not exactly equal to Earth 1G, the differences are not significant enough to make a major impact. Given that, we're going to focus in on how speed has changed Marco

Chung's life."

As Mach went through his explanation, a series of stock photos combined with custom graphics and visual manipulations appeared on screen. Most were not real images of Marco, spaceships, or any such thing, but Mach seemed to feel they were representative enough for his purposes. Mach's own avatar often popped in to provide additional commentary and interact with the illustrations.

Jumping ahead to the relevant details, Mach commenced, "Our story begins when Marco Chung was just eighteen years old. Having never left Earth before, he and everyone on the planet were aging at the same rate. When Marco took the space elevator into orbit and boarded a vessel, though, it was in an era before Quantum Ships even existed. Instead, there were nothing but Torch Ships.

"Okay, we already need to take a little aside. The way the Torch Drive works is that it burns a massive amount of fuel to create thrust, and that thrust simulates gravity by going faster and faster at a rate equal to Earth's gravity, that being 9.8 meters per second squared. What that does mean, though, is that you have to keep adding speed in order to continue to create that same amount of downward pressure that feels like gravity. That's why all spaceships are designed to look like tall buildings; because, as you are moving forward from the perspective of the nose, the 'gravity' is pushing you towards the floor, or the floor towards you, whatever, it doesn't matter!

"Eventually, if you go far enough, you'll reach velocities that can be measured against the speed of light. In other words, you might go 0.25c, or 25% the speed of light! The ship will keep accelerating until it reaches the midpoint of the journey where it must turn off the Torch Drive and literally flip the engine around to the other side. While that is happening, gravity disappears and everyone starts to float, so you and everything else better be strapped in!

"With the Torch Drive on the other side, it relights and uses the same calculations to start slowing itself down. This braking will again feel like 1G of pressure for those inside until they reach their destination. Once there, their velocity will be near zero and they can enter orbit.

"Now, you are probably saying, 'Mach, that

seems like it would take a lot of power!' And you are right. Luckily for Marco, generations earlier humanity had learned to harness energy by combining a variety of techniques together, as well as figure out a way to vent the heat away from the ship so the people inside did not just become crispy nuggets."

At this mention, a graphic of a blackened nugget with eyeballs popped up from the bottom of the screen, blinked a couple of times, and then left the way it had come.

"Even with nearly infinite fire," Mach's returning voiceover noted, "humanity's expansion to the stars was thwarted by one thing: our pesky companion time dilation. Let's look at a typical trip to our nearest neighboring star system Proxima Centauri, which is about 4.3 light-years away. Again, we can't just suddenly start going near the speed of light and get there in about 4.3 years; we have to slowly ramp up the acceleration, get to the halfway point, and slowly decelerate. This means that for someone watching on Earth, the Torch Ship reaches 95% the speed of light at its peak and takes over 5.9 years to reach the system.

"That, though, is not what happens inside the ship. On board, time dilation has made it so that less than 3.6 years have passed for the passengers. Of course, this only includes getting to Proxima Centauri; you have to double it for the return trip. And you must also add in the time actually spent in the system and on the planets there doing the actual work! Marco Chung made two whole trips to the colony on Proxima Centauri B using this archaic method.

"Then, as now, it was rare for someone to take more than even one of these journeys. The roundtrip to Proxima Centauri—assuming a year layover at the colony—would take 12.8 years back on Earth. Yet, because of time dilation, Marco and the other crew members and passengers only experienced the passing of 8.2 years. Even with the longer lifespans we have now compared to our ancestors, 8.2 years is quite a bit. When Marco returned to Earth for the first time, he was over 26 years old. Any same-aged friends he left behind were then nearly 31 years of age. After being gone for so long and literally being slightly out of sync from everyone and everything else makes most people stop right there.

One and done, as the saying goes.

"While uncommon, some people did and still do go out on a second journey. Thus, after a mandatory year back on Earth, no one batted an eye when a still young Marco signed up for a subsequent trip. At the end of that mission, Marco was over 35 years old while, if he had stayed on Earth, he would be approaching 45, a difference of about 9 to 10 years. At that time, people expected that Marco and people like him would then settle back down on Earth.

"In practice, it was and still is commonplace for an HSA crewperson to take a half-journey where they go out to a colony and settle there. Some people find too much has changed for them while they have been away, especially if they partook in two trips like Marco did. This is exceptionally pertinent for those who went out even further than Proxima Centauri.

"Because of the health necessity of staying around 1G and minimizing weightlessness and lesser or greater gravities, that one factor determined just how far it was reasonable for an explorer and potential colonist to go. As such, HSA limited the search radius to just 30 light-years around Earth in every direction. If someone were to do a trip to the edge of that field and return back to Sol, a minimum of 64 years would have passed on Earth, plus whatever time they spent wherever they were going. For the travelers who returned, though, it would have been just 14 years, plus, again, whatever time they may have spent doing studies or setting up a colony. Those addition 50 years that would pass on Earth in their absence would create an insurmountable gap, basically meaning they had left their old lives behind forever!

"More so, in that radius, there are only 17 G-type stars, yellow ones like our sun Sol. If you need to know why that is important, we did an earlier video on this very topic."

In the upper right-hand corner of the screen a box appeared that must have connected to the other video that Mach described. The card was a stationary image of Mach giving two thumbs down to a planet in the background and indicated the linked video was entitled "Why Proxima Centauri B is the Worst Colony".

With the advertisement to the other video still hanging above his pointing avatar, Mach said, "Click the link onscreen now to learn about that. In a nutshell, planets circling close to red dwarf stars are not great—to say the least—so it was decided that efforts should be focused on rocky bodies around sun-like stars.

"Using telescopes in our home system and sending robotic missions to the exoplanets can only tell you so much, though. To really know for sure if we can possibly set up a colony and terraform a raw planet, we have to go there and see it with our own eyes. And perhaps even more important than that, human hands and minds are necessary in the search for signs of present or past life. Just because none has been found yet doesn't mean it's not out there!

"After some earlier exploratory missions proved fruitless both in the search for life and potential colonies, the criteria were further narrowed from G-type stars to ones that were very close to 1 solar mass—in other words, the size of Sol. Of the 17 G-type stars, this eliminated half of them right off the top. Then, based on the experience at Proxima Centauri B, scientists deemed that only very close Earth-analogues should be further investigated, planets where the size and gravity were almost equal to Earth and were located in a much tighter habitable zone than was considered before. Given all of these factors, that really only left a couple of places to physically go to and test out.

"As such, an exploratory mission was being organized to Delta Pavonis, which is about 19.9 light-years away from Earth. The roundtrip, including the planned two years to be spent in the system conducting experiments, would last almost 46 Earth-years and 14 for the crew. In other words, it was the equivalent of several missions unto itself. That is why HSA was completely shocked when Marco Chung volunteered."

Snippets of a document were shown on screen that contained emails between HSA administrators discussing the pros and cons of allowing Marco to go on this mission. In the end, they decided that his experience would be too invaluable to deny him the opportunity to join the expedition.

After reviewing these documents and some details about the operation, Mach continued his soliloquy. "Following the Delta Pavonis assignment, Marco returned to Earth having lived through 50 years on his own personal clock while the planet had spun around the Sun over 91 times since his birth. Unfortunately, Marco had to contend with the fallout of the mission being a complete failure. There were no signs of past or present life and the only potential planet in the system proved completely unsuitable for a long-term human colony. Whereas Marco was mostly anonymous before this trip, his return brought him into the spotlight, which included shouldering part of the blame. While Marco never attempted to defend himself in public, others did, noting all that he sacrificed to try to make the endeavor a success. It seemed like after giving so much to the Human Expansion Program, Marco Chung was going to retire from it a pariah.

"But what a difference a year makes! A mission was heading out to the first, and at that time, only successful colony around a G-type star at Eta Cassiopeiae A, 19.4 light-years away. HSA allowed Marco to join the operation, but the consensus was that this was going to be his retirement cruise. Everyone assumed he was just flying the half trip and would settle into his solitude out on the colony now known as 'Eden 2', away from the scornful eyes back on Earth. Boy, were they surprised when just over 43 years after leaving, Marco landed back on Earth having lived 64 years from his frame of reference compared to the nearly 136 that had passed on Earth.

"HSA was not pleased to see Marco again. He had become a symbol of the organization's failures. Although Eta Cassiopeiae A and its planet Eden 2 were a roaring success, the disappointments that culminated with Delta Pavonis emphasized one thing: humanity was trapped. They had run out of reasonable options within a 30-light-year radius and needed to start thinking about new possibilities while also keeping the public hopeful about the future and the program.

"Because of that, they decided to push the boundaries. A promising world was spotted around Delta Trianguli A, 35.4 light-years away. With the 3-year exploration and colonization component included, the mission would be over 77 Earth-years—which was at that time about three-quarters of a lifetime. Perhaps just to get rid of him, Marco was allowed to join this expedition, too. Unfortunately for all involved, a then nearly 83-year-old Marco Chung returned to

Earth as a two-time loser over 214 years after his birth. The curse seemed real."

The image on screen changed to some gloomy-faced meme that must have been popular when the video was made. There was no explanation as to the frame of reference, so it is impossible to say if it was even well-known by the potential viewers of this video.

"While he was away," the returning Mach chimed in, "something amazing happened. Just five years after Marco and the crew left, the Quantum Shift breakthrough was made! After dealing with the initial accident during its discovery, the process was refined and the rules were created so that the technology could be safely implemented and applied to interstellar travel. In short order, the Quantum Drive and the Quantum Ships were created and a whole new exploration and colonization program began with renewed vigor!

"Sadly for Marco Chung and his crew, no one bothered to tell them! Instead of using one of the first missions to go out there and let them know about this revolutionary development, HSA decided it would be more economical to allow them to complete their mission as intended and use the freed-up resources for new exploration and colonization. Further, there were no data repeaters between systems in that era; and there certainly would not be any way out on the frontier even if they had been deployed elsewhere. Thus, it was completely impractical to even attempt to send them a message. By the time the message would have been received, they'd be well on their way home. Marco and his crew did not learn that they had completely wasted their time until they came down to Puerta Estrella.

"For the next three years, it seemed like Marco's spacefaring days were over. Throughout the decades that contained Marco's adventures, aside from the technological leaps in space navigation, many advances were made in the healthcare field—especially in the area of longevity. Upon each of his returns, Marco partook in every single one of these to further extend his life. Regrettably, many of these treatments needed to be taken earlier on in order to not only extend one's life, but to suppress and sometimes reverse the aging process itself. Doctors have done all they can for Marco Chung, but he will always look significantly older than he actually is. Of course, all the exposure to radiation in the deep dark has certainly not helped the situation.

"Still, because of these treatments, even at around 85 of his personal years old, he was considered relatively middle-aged. That is when he decided to forgo all his rank and status and start over again, this time as a member of the Quantum Ship Fleet!"

Some type of musical overture started playing that was perhaps the anthem of the Quantum Ship Fleet. A picture of a Quantum Ship was shown on screen with an unidentifiable flag fluttering behind it. Numerous cartoon and video game characters from a variety of properties were saluting the ship and flag from the bottom of the screen.

"As such," Mach said as the musical rendition came to an abrupt end, "Marco headed out on his first quantum expedition as a lowly deckhand. This time, though, the trip would be much, much, much quicker than his last trek. Every single quantum trip runs for 7.8 Earth-years and 6.2 years from the crew's perspective. That is because even though we call them 'Quantum Ships', they are actually a hybrid of classic 'Torch Drives' and the 'Quantum Shift Effect'. In all situations, the ships use the Torch Drive to fly one light-year away from whatever planet they started at, engage the Quantum Drive, appear one light-year from their destination, and then start the flipping and deceleration process. In other words, every voyage is technically just two light-years long.

"By the way, earlier I said the energy available for Torch Ships was nearly infinite. Well, that was a teensy-weensy little lie. It looks like it is infinite from our viewpoint, but there are some very real limitations that HSA scientists and engineers take into account. The Quantum Ships only need to reach 87% the speed of light, so the energy savings compared to a stand-alone Torch Ship are massive! Needing less fuel means that they don't have to carry that excess weight. Due to that, they can instead bring more people and cargo with them, which has helped hasten the development of the colonization program.

"Anyway, typically, crews only spend a year at their destinations, whether it is a supply, exploratory, settlement, or some other kind of mission. Some of this layover has to do with the time to refuel the ship, as well as repair the engines from the natural wear-and-tear of actually using them. Either way, this has standardized many facets of the job that it lacked compared to when Marco first set out. Despite this, as highlighted before, most people still only do one or two of these missions. The dilation only amounts to a year and half, but the feeling of disconnect and isolation has been well documented by psychologists. A rather large percentage of crew members take an extra half trip and settle on a colony because they cannot deal with being out of sync relative to those they left behind.

"Still, it is not as if this will be the last time their friends and family on Earth will ever see them! Everyone who returns to Earth, including crew members like Marco Chung, are required to spend an entire year planet-side. For some reason, all humans—especially those who were born in the colonies, whether in the Sol System or in some extrasolar system—need to make at least one pilgrimage to the home world in their lifetime in consideration of their overall health. Oftentimes, multiple sabbaticals are necessary.

Doctors do not really understand why, but being enveloped in Earth's biosphere for a spell is essential for the effectiveness of the longevity treatments. The results are quite clear and measurable. Therefore, even though many people leave, they do have to come back for a long visit every once in a while in order to get the full benefits of their longevity treatment.

"HSA is particularly sensitive to this situation, so even the rare few individuals like Marco Chung who want to keep going out on missions must spend a year or more on Earth before heading out again.

"And keep going out Marco did! In total, including his most recent roundtrip to Novissimus, he has been on eleven Quantum Ship missions, more than anyone in existence! Although he started over at the bottom, he quickly rose back up through the ranks to being a captain. Marco is now considered the foremost expert on Torch and Quantum Ship functionality, as well as the technologies that keep colonies operational.

"Now, all of that background information we have gone through was necessary in order to bring us back to our original question of just how old is Marco Chung? Without further ado...”

But there was further ado as a long drumroll ensued with many false snare indicators that it was over. After over a minute and a half of this, there was a pop and graphics of confetti flowing all over the screen as the numbers appeared.

Highlighting those numerals, Mach said, “Marco Chung has lived almost 164 years by his own clock while 316 years have passed on Earth!”

An artificial audience cheered, oohed and aahed, and clapped in excitement. Mach accepted these platitudes without any semblance of modesty, basking in the moment before deciding to come back and wrap up his main thesis.

“Although humans can potentially live to a couple of hundred, maybe even 250 years now,” concluded Mach, “that most likely won’t be Marco Chung’s fate. He was born too far back, before these spans were even remotely possible. Unfortunately, his time may be coming to an end sooner rather than later. Yes, he could live for decades more, and who knows what advancements in longevity may be made in that time that could help him? Out in the colonies in particular, they are pursuing this path as they try to find ways to be less dependent upon Earth and needing to pause their lives for eight years just to improve the treatments' success rates. Thus, something may be in the process of being discovered as we speak! Still, I want to be realistic about Marco's future. All signs indicate that he wants to go out on another mission, so realistically, he'll probably die out there at some point— whether it's the next journey or the one after that or even the one after that one. And perhaps that is what he wants!

"Afterall, there is no one else who is alive from when Marco was born. He has no family, no known descendants of his own, no one he is connected to. Owing to his limited time spent anywhere that was not in outer space, he does not even have a close network of friends. To him, almost everyone is a complete stranger."

RECORD #06: SPEED

By this point, you should now have a pretty decent understanding about how the Quantum Drive functions, at least at a high level. Just to clarify, even though we call it a "drive", it is really an "effect". When engaged, we are not going "quantum speed" or traversing some "quantum corridor" or even jumping through a "wormhole". The "Quantum Shift" is not a speed or a velocity or even a movement as we would define it in classical physics.

Instead, we use another quirk of quantum physics to create a supermassive quantum computer that, with the help of artificial intelligence, does the simultaneous calculations and work for us. If we attempted to do the same thing with linear computers like the ones we use every day in our normal lives, it would take a trillion times the entire age of the universe to even do a small part of the job. Basically, we turn quantum principles on themselves by making some elementary particles turn into observers and force their comrades to collapse their waves into a specific location. However, instead of just looking where we are, we force the observation to be where we want to go. This is why the official name is the "Quantum Probability Shift Wave Collapse Observer Effect". Since that rolls right off the tongue, we just say "Quantum Effect" or "Quantum Shift" for short, and "Quantum Drive" to describe what we do with spacefaring vessels.

So, how does the computer doing these calculations limit it to just the Quantum Ship and everything inside of it? In short, it does not.

We cannot actually see the size and shape of the "field"—for lack of a better word—that the Quantum Drive generates around the ship. At best, we guess it is some type of amorphous, irregular blob; but we really aren't sure. What we do know, though, is that it does extend beyond the ship and also takes all of those particles floating out there with it.

Many people like to think that outer space is empty, but it isn't; it is just far less dense in terms of matter than on a planet. If you were to create a box that was 1 cubic meter, about 1,000 liters if filled with a liquid, and drop it off in the intergalactic medium, you would still find a handful of particles in there. If you did the same on Earth, you would discover several factors of billions more particles. Although there are not a lot of crumbs the further you get away from a celestial body or structure, there is always something nearby.

And we, unfortunately, have a pretty good example of this impact in action. An early-concept experiment that was testing the potential of the Quantum Effect was taking place in labs located on the dwarf planetoid Ceres, located in the Asteroid Belt between Mars and Jupiter. When the Quantum Drive prototype was activated, its field was completely uncontrollable and took itself, the lab, almost all of the researchers, and a decent chunk of Ceres with it. The environmental breach caused by this accident led to a catastrophic failure, destroying the entire colony in the end and killing hundreds of thousands of people. Then, resulting from this disaster, there was an uncontrollable chain reaction in the Asteroid Belt that ended up taking out a couple of spinning asteroid colonies and sent debris flying in every direction. Even hundreds of years later, we are still dealing with the fallout.

The scientists simply did not understand how big the field could get, or that there was a field at all to keep track of. Although we still do not have the answers, we are much better at controlling field shape and breadth, per se. A lot of it has to do with the quantum computing power we can harness. Thus, as our computing capabilities have increased, so has the general size of the field. This has led to two things.

First off, the magnitude of field is one of the limiting factors for how big a Quantum Ship can get (along with the fuel needed for classical Torch Drive maneuvers, but more on this in a moment). The field we can create now is much larger than the one that took out part of the colony on Ceres. Which brings us to the second point: theoretically these fields could get much, much bigger. Next generation Quantum Ships are expected to have computing power far beyond their field size needs, and there might be ways to expand that even more. One day, we could possibly be able to move objects the size of the Earth itself! Imagine that as the sun physically expands in diameter towards becoming a red giant that we could move Venus, Earth/Luna, and Mars further back so the planets remain viable! That is the ultimate potential of this technology.

But we are a long, long way from that being a possibility. In many ways, the rapid advancements that were made between the discovery of the Quantum Drive and the creation of the Quantum Ship have stalled out. Sure, there have been some incremental improvements, but overall things have really stagnated. Based on our current capabilities and where the technology is right now, if we tried to extend the field too much, we would probably lose control of where the wave collapsed. Potentially, it might even make the wave materialize over a wide range. Thus, if you took a ball, it would reappear as a flat disc spread out over a massive distance.

I know this all sounds quite alarming, but you really don't need to be worrying about any of that! No one is attempting to do anything like that right now, especially not within one light-year of any planet. Because of what happened on Ceres, the technology became tightly controlled.

Nowadays, Quantum Ships are only built in the Sol System with compartmentalized knowledge of the principles and methodologies that make them work. The law stipulates that there are very few people in existence who could possibly know the entire functionality end-to-end; most personnel involved only have a small piece of the puzzle. Even yours truly does not know that much, but I am happy to share with you what I can.

Yet I must be careful with my own words as there are severe penalties for revealing excessive details to the public at large or trying to learn too much on your own. This is particularly true in the extrasolar colonies. Those people are forbidden from pursing even the general concepts, and this is enforced through rather draconian methods. While it feels unfair to many—especially to explorers that want to use their colonies as jumping off points for exploration to further out destinations and expansion so they are not so dependent upon Earth—these laws are for everyone's safety. Imagine if what happened on Ceres took place on a colony like Eden 2 with its tens of millions of citizens. No one wants something dangerous like a "quantum bomb" going off in a cradle of humanity!

Because of these laws, even the captains of Quantum Ships do not really comprehend how they get their crafts to do the job. When I interviewed Marco Chung for this very book, he could describe how to engage the effect and what it felt like, but not what was happening. He told me that he always experienced it as "a slight dizziness, but not a movement. Everything is just out of focus for the briefest of moments, and then it is not."

Although there are very few people who understand how the technology operates in totality, one does not need to know how something works in order to use it in a hazardous way. After all, you do not need to be a nuclear physicist to drop a weapon of mass destruction on an unsuspecting populous.

That is why trustworthy people like Marco Chung are so critical to the Human Expansion Program. They take their Quantum Ships one light-year out in order to make sure they are safely far away from anything they could possibly damage. Then, they shift their location to one light-year from where they are going for the same reason. Even though the field's size and form are uncontrollable and mostly unknowable, at that distance there is very little for us to be concerned about. The crew's sacrifice of years away—along with how many of them suffer from time-dilation disconnect syndrome—is necessary to ensure the safety and future of all humankind.

RECORD #07: HISTORY
INTERVIEW SEGMENT, POSSIBLY EDITED

"Our guest for this hour," Veronica Dubois told the in-studio audience, "needs no introduction, but I am going to give him one anyway. He is a personal hero of mine, someone directly responsible for the Human Expansion Program, and just so happens to be the oldest person in the universe. Everyone, please welcome Captain Macro Chung of the HSA Quantum Drive Fleet!"

And welcome him the crowd did. As Marco came out from behind a curtain—obviously uncomfortable with all of the attention and noise—the audience got to its feet to clap, cheer, whistle, and whoop. Even after Marco sat down in the plush chair adjacent to Veronica, the raucousness continued for nearly another minute. Finally, Veronica signaled for everyone to quiet down so that she could continue the segment.

"Marco, Captain Chung, that was quite the ovation you just got." Veronica began. "I don't think I've ever seen anything like it on our set!"

"Just Marco is fine, please," Marco demurred. "I'm not much for formalities. Well, ahh, thank you everyone, I suppose. That was all, rather... unexpected."

"But well deserved," Veronica crooned. "You are an icon, a hero, to these people; to me, too. I was so excited to see you at the Interstellar Parade a couple of months ago, and here you are now on my show! I just want to tell you that what you have so gallantly done for your entire adult life is appreciated by me and everyone here; really, everyone everywhere."

Marco's expression did not change from its outwardly and seemingly usual grimace, but he cast his eyes downward as he said, "I'm no great hero. I didn't do any of this for altruism. Once upon a time, all I was looking for was a way to escape my terrible life and make some money. That is all that motivated me to get off this rock."

Veronica momentarily seemed taken aback, but she quickly gathered herself and made sure her authentic smile stayed plastered on her face. "Well, yes, it must have been tough for you, with the way you grew up. You were born in an orphanage?"

"Not born there," Marco corrected. "I had parents once, or so I am told. They died when I was very young, too young to remember. I never really found out what happened to them, or really anything about them. If there ever were records, with all the global upheavals that have happened over my lifetime, the documents seem to have simply been lost."

Veronica's eyebrows scrunched in a quizzical manner. She leaned in closer to Marco in a conspiratorial position, asking, "But you must know something about them. Your last name, Chung, I would think that your father was Chinese then?"

"Hmmm, maybe," Marco considered. "I took some DNA tests and whatnot and they came back as part Chinese, part Spanish, part indigenous to Ecuador, and many parts other things. I don't really think of myself in terms of those ethnicities, though."

"Oh," inquired Veronica, "how do you identify and define yourself?"

Marco's stare pierced straight through Veronica for several moments and she shifted uncomfortably in her own plush chair, crossing her legs the other way. Finally, Marco seemed to realize he had not spoken out loud and said the words he was thinking. "You don't even know what a strange question that is. It is so very Earth-centric to think in terms like ethnicities and nations and other artificial barriers. All of these labels are meaningless, especially in the grand scope of the cosmos."

Veronica tried to interject but Marco would not let her. "Veronica, if you asked someone who was born on any colony that same question, no matter if it was far away Novissimus or next-door Venus, they would have almost no idea what you were talking about. They don't know the land masses and political borders back on Earth; these are foreign concepts of some far-away place they'll perhaps see once in their life-times. They don't mean anything and therefore I don't think about them."

Appearing to sense that she had raised Marco's ire and wanting to lower the tension, Veronica shifted the questioning in another direction. "I get it, that makes a lot of sense. I'd like to, then, ask you a little bit about growing up in that orphanage, if that is alright?" Veronica did not wait to hear the answer to her inquiry as she jumped right in asking, "It was in Puerta Estrella, correct?"

Marco quickly got over his whiplash and said, "Yes, but not the Puerta Estrella you see nowadays. When I was a kid, it was a much smaller town, one cloaked in the shadow of Volcán Cayambe. Over the course my many journeys, I watched it grow into a massive metropolitan sprawl, then I saw it fall into urban decay."

Veronica put her hand over Marco's and said, "It must have been hard for you, to see your hometown change so much, and not always for the better."

"I've seen the same thing happen many times on many different worlds," Marco retorted. "A village becomes a town, a town becomes a city, a city becomes a megalopolis, and all the while its core starts to rot from the inside out. It's like the universe hates everything we have built and is constantly trying to tear it down."

Removing her hand, Veronica asked, "You mean like entropy? The natural force in the universe that is always trying to push towards disorder and diffusion?"

Marco thought for a moment and a smirk

quickly flashed across his face before returning to its typical forbearance. "Yes," he said, "yes, I suppose you could think of it like that. But I've seen enough to know it is something more."

"I believe I understand," Veronica declared. Whether she did or not is debatable, but apparently proclaiming she understood the deeper meaning appeared to be enough to satisfy this line of questioning as she continued the interview. "Were you close to anyone at the orphanage? Any of the other kids or the administrators? Are you in contact with any of their descendants?"

"No, Veronica," began Marco, "I was only trying to survive. I know this all happened before your grandparents were born and is hard to understand, but the world—the universe—I came from was entirely different."

"In what way?" Veronica asked.

Marco was silent for a moment before continuing. "Earth was already overpopulated and then we started to break the code to longevity. Yes, you all laugh at the standard lifespans we could coble together back then, but it seemed like a long time compared to what people even a couple of generations before could muster. Because of this, we were superfluous. Earth didn't need more people, especially unwanted children who couldn't offer anything. Resources for us were limited. The people in charge and supposedly watching over us didn't really want to be there, either. It was a miserable existence."

"I am so sorry," Veronica conceded, "I had no idea. You've never disclosed anything like this before."

"Well, I am a very private person," Marco admitted.

"They why tell us now?"

Marco sighed before resuming. "Veronica, I am dying. Not today, not tomorrow, probably not anytime soon, but it will happen eventually. The realization of that simple truth and acceptance of that fact is freeing."

"So, in other words," Veronica interjected, "you know you aren't going to live forever, and want to make the most of the time you have left?"

"I definitely need to do something—something vital—with my limited remaining years, that's for sure," Marco confessed.

"Then, the rumors are true?" Veronica

probed. "You really are going to go out on another Quantum Ship mission?"

"I see no reason to lie," Marco said. "Assuming I have my way, I will definitely be going out there to do, perhaps, what is really my life's mission. Before I leave this plane of existence, I will ensure its success. That is my duty."

"Such dedication to HSA and the Human Expansion Program!" Veronica declared. "How did this come to be? You were barely eighteen years old when you left on your first mission."

"When you turn eighteen," Marco grumbled, "the system considers you an adult. You are on your own. When an opportunity became available, I snatched it up. I just wanted—needed—to get away as quickly as possible."

Veronica held her hands over her chest and gasped, "I think you are glossing over quite a bit of your own history here!"

"Oh?" inquired Marco, his curiosity evidently finally piqued. "Why don't you tell me what I went through?"

A bit taken aback, Veronica summarized, "Well, I don't want to speak for you, but there were some amazing happenstances. The Torch

Ship was set to be boarded in just a few days and was already fully staffed. Then, one of the crewmembers was found severely beaten, and suddenly there was an open spot that needed to be immediately filled."

"As I said before," Marco interrupted, "these cities overflow with desolation. Puerta Estrella was not a safe place for anyone, especially outsiders. They could have just wandered into the wrong part of town or it could have been a robbery gone wrong. Who knows?"

"That's true, no one really does; the case was never solved," Veronica conceded. "Although they were brought to the hospital, they died a few weeks later."

"I vaguely remember hearing about that when I returned from my mission, so many years later," Marco said with an almost perplexed expression as he tried to recall the details. "I never knew them, no one on the crew had even met them yet. They might have just been trying to run away like me and had no one else in the whole world, either."

"It would seem so," Veronica agreed. "Nevertheless, this tragedy opened a door for you."

"That's luck for you," Marco granted. "I happened to be there, I didn't have anything going on, I wanted to get the hell out of where I was at, and I had nothing keeping me earthbound."

"But didn't you know some people who worked for the space complex?" Veronica asked.

Marco quickly shot back, "Of course, of course, everyone in that town knew someone who worked there in some fashion or another. The second I heard they were looking for a deckhand seat-filler, I asked everyone I knew to put my name in. I guess I was literally the first person in the door, so they picked me and I signed my contract right then and there."

"Wow," Veronica exclaimed, "what an astounding concurrence. And that set you on the path to becoming the oldest man in human history!"

"Believe me," Marco responded, "it was never my goal. However, I came aboard a snot nosed punk and have spent the decades bettering myself. Oh, not right away, no. Those first couple of trips I squandered the opportunities I was given. I philandered, gambled, fought, you name it. But somewhere along the line I realized I could use all of that downtime on the long journeys to actually learn and be useful. Now I understand."

"You really have become the foremost expert in the field," Veronica reflected, "even just by osmosis alone due to all of the experiences and knowledge you've been exposed to over the years. But I'm sure there are things you don't know, and things that by law you're not allowed to know."

This actually got a laugh out of Marco and Veronica took it as an opportunity to investigate deeper. "Do tell me, Marco, after your long, storied career, did you ever consider settling down at one of the colonies? After all, you helped build several of them and you made trips out to even more. Surely you could have found somewhere that tickled your fancy?"

If Veronica thought she had made some headway, this question appeared to set things rapidly spiraling backwards. Returning to his standard gloomy disposition, Marco proclaimed, "No, Veronica, none of those colonies were for me. Puerta Estrella, Ecuador, Earth, the entire Sol System—none of them feels like home. The extrasolar colonies are even worse."

"That is quite a shocking statement coming from someone such as yourself!" Veronica chimed in.

"I'm only speaking for myself," Marco retorted, "not anyone else. Surviving on the colonies is no picnic, either. The constant battle against nature, the totalitarianism in the name of safety and security, the forced dependency on others—none of that is for me."

Veronica's shell cracked and she showed actual concern. "Are you recommending people not immigrate to the colonies?"

Marco was quick to retract this, like he had been caught committing a crime. "No, no, no, no! No, that is not what I am saying at all. It is just that people need to realize that every day in a colony is a struggle just to keep the settlement from imploding. Sometimes, though, it makes you wonder if trying to spread humanity to the stars was just a big mistake."

Record #08: Co-workers
Clips from an In-Progress Documentary

"Quantum Drive Ships," the voiceover narrator began as a drone video swept around an example of that type of vessel, "are an intentional enigma to most everyone. Only a handful of people truly completely understand how they function, but this does not stop hundreds of people from serving aboard them for over six years of their life at a time, which is equivalent to almost eight years back at their point of origin.

"For the ten-thousand or so passengers traveling one way or another, their single-direction journey only lasts a little over two and half years of their own time, or close to three and a half from whence they came. Sharing space aboard the ship with them are massive amounts of cargo containing resources that are especially vital to the extrasolar colonies. Critical materials, supplies, and knowhow are all exported from Earth outwards towards the rest of the galaxy, with only a fraction coming back in return. Without regular deliveries, the colonies would surely collapse, as even the oldest are unable to sustain themselves completely."

At this, the film changed scenes from the Quantum Ship to drone sweeps over various settlements on other worlds. While the documentarians appeared to be implying this was all original work, a look through the base files quickly confirmed that thus far all of the vistas used came from clearinghouses that made generic clips available for a licensing fee. While high quality, they were not necessarily created for the purposes being presented here.

As the narrator quieted down, Marco Chung emerged on the screen. He appeared to be sitting in front of some controls on the bridge of a Quantum Ship and was explaining the general size, layout, and other technical features of the spacecraft. Everything he was saying was quite dry and stilted, as if just talking into the camera lens was painful.

The view shifted again, this time to hallways and open areas aboard a ship on a mission in progress. The tops of passengers' heads were shown going this way and that as the narrator returned and said, "Individuals like Captain Marco Chung of the HSA Quantum Ship Fleet are responsible for making sure all of these precious people and freight safely reach their destination, and then doing the same for anyone and anything heading back to Earth. Our film crew was given unprecedented access to document a mission to Novissimus, and most importantly, the members of the crew that make the Human Expansion Program possible. This is their story."

A note in the file stated that they were waiting for their composer to finish producing the score that would play over the opening credits. As such, the introduction consisting of a computer animated Quantum Ship traveling between worlds and spreading mankind like it was planting flowers was completely silent. Several more notes were found in the metadata questioning some of the choices shown in the cold open and whether the filmmakers had successfully made it clear what this documentary was supposed to be about and if they had truly captured the viewers' attentions. One reviewer in particular was concerned that if they did not do something exciting in the first 20 seconds, they would lose half of their audience instantly.

There was then a gap in the file as whatever segment they were planning to place there was apparently incomplete. Instead, after a short period of blackness, the film suddenly cut to the next component.

The scene began with an unidentified crewman facing the camera in a closeup shot that cut off his forehead and chin. "Captain Chung?" he stuttered. "Oh, um, that's an interesting question. I mean, he is excellent at what he does, really. It's just..."

As he trailed off, the narrator returned to introduce a different crewmember named Ravee Schmitt. Assumingly, the missing sequence was about HSA contractors on their first journey as this segment was about those who were heading out on at least their second trip.

The narrator finished discussing Ravee's background and details about her first mission. At this, Ravee started speaking as she tucked her hair behind her ears. "I mean, most of the people here are on their first and only tour. Even though we spend years together, we try not to get too close. I made that mistake on my first mission...

Her name was Becca, but she was only taking a half-trip. I had years alone after she was gone to reflect on that mistake.

"I guess I was still distressed about that when I returned to Earth. At first, I wasn't planning on going out into space again. Let's be real: you do this job for the money. We get paid a hell of a lot to basically be babysitters for six years. That money was supposed to be a nest egg for what I really wanted to do with the rest of my life."

"What was that?" a muffled voice behind the camera asked as the same words appeared below Ravee on the screen.

Ravee was quiet for a moment. She then brushed her fingers under her eye, tilted her head back, and laughed. "You know what," she snickered, "I don't even remember anymore!"

Showing action shots around the ship, the narrator explained that this was a common occurrence among the returning crewmembers. "At first," said the narrator, "they thought that they would take their money and run. But for some reason, it just did not work out that way for all of them. They were never able to settle back into their old lives they had left behind, so they decided to re-up their contracts. HSA actually pays even more for experience, a scale that grows exponentially with each journey."

With that, the story returned to Ravee. A note in the file asked if they shouldn't cut to someone else for variety, at least for a while. There was a response in agreement and a request for a particular person to hunt for an appropriate piece to put in this slot. They must not have gotten the chance to do so because the Ravee module was still inserted there.

"This is your third mission?" prompted the person behind the camera. "Also, your second with Captain Chung?"

"Yes," Ravee replied, "I served with Marco on my second mission, too. In all honesty, I was inspired by him. I went out the second time just because I had to get away from Earth again; I was completely out of sync. When I signed up, it was only for a half journey, I was going to get off at the colony. They let you do that, you know. If you do one full tour, they let you take a half trip to settle out at a colony. A lot of people do that. Or, they do a second trip to make a bunch more money and then a half trip after that. Most people I talk to say they'll be better off starting over off-world. I can understand that; I thought the same thing.

"But serving with Marco showed me that I could make a permanent life out here, wandering the stars forever. When I returned to Earth that first time, I was so uneasy with just how different everything had become. Talking with Marco, though, made me realize how changed and uncomfortable life back on Earth can be for people like us. If that's what I felt after one trip, can you imagine what he must think about the home world and its people? Or even the colonies he's been able to visit multiple times?"

"Did you ever consider trying to find Becca again, and settle down on her colony?" asked the disembodied voice.

"That bitch," Ravee laughed. "No, no, I've had enough time to know that that wouldn't have worked either."

The narrator chimed in at this declaration and stated, "Not everyone agrees with Ravee's viewpoint."

At this point, the scene returned to the previously nameless crewperson. This time, a chyron at the bottom of the screen identified him as Tiyamike Okafor and highlighted that he was on a half mission after completing his first.

"I am so looking forward to finally getting off this tin can," declared Tiyamike. "I've made a lot of money, and I'm ready to at long last use it to start a real life."

"But you weren't able to do that on Earth?" the offscreen voice asked.

"Oh, I could, I could," Tiyamike avowed, "but there are better opportunities on the colonies."

"Did you feel any symptoms of time-dilation disconnect syndrome back on Earth?" the voice questioned.

This inquiry seemed to greatly tickle Tiyamike. Laughing, he said, "Oh, no, no, no—I felt fine. I don't really believe that is a thing, anyway. People who believe in that junk, they just need an excuse, so they got one that they can get a diagnosis and a prescription for."

"And you find that amusing?" the voice wanted to know.

"No, no, not that, it's just that your question, it got me thinking more about Captain Chung..."

"What about him?"

"People bitch about not being in sync, but talking with that guy is like speaking with a real-life alien. Yeah, for me, a fair bunch of years had passed on Earth, but I still generally knew what was going on. The people I grew up with, my family, we had the same memories from before. All our references were the same, you understand?"

When the documentarian did not respond, Tiyamike continued, "Well Captain Chung, he's a man out of time—he doesn't get any references, any jokes, he doesn't get anything! And if he had any of his own, I wouldn't get them, either. Thankfully, I guess, he doesn't seem to have anything to reference to begin with; he's all work, like a robot, all aloof. There's nothing there to talk about, unless you want to learn about the nuances of quantum theory, and I don't."

At this, the ethereal voice pondered, "Is there anything you do admire about Captain Chung?"

"Oh, oh, I don't mean to disrespect him," insisted Tiyamike. "He really is great at the job, and he's a good boss in many ways. He's never overbearing and basically lets us do anything we want so long as we don't neglect the ship's maintenance. Plus, I'm kinda jealous of him."

"How so?" the voice queried.

Tiyamike did not hesitate. "He has so much wealth! After all of these journeys and years of compounding interest, can you imagine how much money he has? I think I watched a video on it once by that, uh, what's his name? You know, that Cosmic Questions thing... no, wait, that <u>Cosmic Quandaries</u> guy. Yeah, that's it. Anyway, he calculated that Marco must have a GDP bigger than some countries and even entire colonies! If Marco wanted to, he could probably buy his own private army!"

RECORD #09: COURT

The Holy Church of the Sixth Day Reclamation—more commonly known as the "Sixth Day Cult" or the "Sixth Dayers"—scored a major victory in court this morning. The Human Space Agency (HSA) was seeking to have a temporary restraining order extended into a permanent one, but instead found their original plea completely struck down.

The issue began during the "Interstellar Parade" in Puerta Estrella, Ecuador, Earth when members of the Sixth Day Cult took part in a purportedly violent riot. The perpetrators were quickly dispersed and later apprehended, but an emergency restraining order was granted that forced all adherents to keep away from the parade and the festival that followed. After that, HSA sued to have the separation between the two organizations made permanent and remove the Sixth Dayers from the general vicinity of the space elevator landing and within the municipal borders of Puerta Estrella specifically. The judge assigned to the case agreed to a temporary restraining order within 100 meters of the space elevator landing and any HSA offices and facilities while arguments were heard, but refused to make any further concessions in favor of the plaintiffs.

Over the course of the trial, HSA filed multiple requests for expanding the scope of the temporary edict. Director of the Human Space Agency David Clarke claimed that the Sixth Dayers had been a constant disrupting force to their operations and that their very presence was an implied threat to the safety of everyone involved in the Human Expansion Program. Director Clarke further stated that in his capacity as leader of HSA, he had tried to remain tolerant of the Sixth Dayers, but that leniency had only emboldened them.

While under questioning, Mr. Clarke said, "I now believe it was a mistake to try to be reasonable with these terrorists, and the time is upon us to come down hard on extremism. We must protect the Human Expansion Program at all costs because it is unequivocally the most important undertaking for all mankind, both right now and into the foreseeable future."

The judge appeared quite unconvinced by this line of reasoning. During cross-examination, the judge disagreed with Mr. Clarke that the Human Expansion Program was a requirement of any kind, and stated that his assertion was just his personal perspective, and a political one at that. Unambiguously, the judge said, "Although it [the Human Expansion Program] enjoys wide popularity in the here and now, polls show that to be fading somewhat. Do you concede that, in time, perhaps, the Sixth Dayers could be in the majority and HSA, consequently, would be in the minority?"

Director Clarke did grant that that could be a possibility, albeit a remote one, but if it did come to pass it would result in an existential crisis. Once again reprimanding the witness that what he contended was an opinion, the judge then asked, "If the shoe were on the other foot, would you want The Holy Church of the Sixth Day Reclamation to say whether or not you could approach the space elevator?"

"Of course not," Director Clarke responded,

"we need access to the space elevator in order to do our job."

In response, the judge queried, "And don't the Sixth Dayers need access to the space elevator to do their job, that being proselytizing to people leaving the planet and attempting to stop them with persuasive arguments?"

This was not the only time the judge showed a lot of skepticism for the arguments HSA was making. For instance, when HSA appealed the conditions of the temporary restraining order—particularly noting that it should be extended to the entirety of Puerta Estrella—the judge identified the fact that HSA does not own the city, it is merely a tenant there. Similarly, the judge highlighted that members of the Sixth Dayers are also residents and the church actually owns quite a bit of property within its boundaries. As such, they had all the same equal rights under the law.

It was the same when the conversation turned towards the space elevator. The judge observed that it is not exclusively HSA property; that they just operate it on behalf of the Terran government and Earth Central Command, the latter of whom are the actual possessors. "The space elevator is very much public land," the judge emphasized.

Speaking on behalf of the Holy Church of the Sixth Day Reclamation for much of the proceedings was their Chief Missionary, who only goes by that honorific. The Chief Missionary told the court that "as part of my station, I gave up my name and am now known only by my title. I live only in service to God and to his holy cause."

On the stand, the Chief Missionary underscored that the Church does not condone the violence that was perpetrated in their name. Further, he stressed that they had excommunicated those individuals from their faith when they learned of their crimes, and, more so, were completely cooperative with law enforcement in identifying the suspects. The Church even provided all of the records they had, which helped lead to swift arrests.

When asked by lawyers for the prosecution if the Church truly preaches nonviolent measures, then why did those members partake in it, the Chief Missionary blamed HSA employees for provoking them. "I am not excusing their actions," the Chief Missionary testified, "but they are not completely at fault, either." These alleged provocations were not spelled out and deemed by the judge to be irrelevant to the case at hand.

In the end, though, the judge found in favor of the Holy Church of the Sixth Day Reclamation and removed the temporary restraining order in its entirety. In her written decision, the judge drew attention to the fact that the Church could not be found liable for the actions of independent persons, even if those people were at one time affiliated with them. Additionally, those individuals were being prosecuted in their own criminal cases and—should they be found guilty—would face appropriate penalties in those courtrooms.

In a statement, HSA said that they respectfully disagreed with the judge's ruling and were weighing their options. Otherwise, they had no further comment at this time.

Record #10: Math

Is there other life out in the universe beyond Earth? Thus far, we haven't found any. Probability tells us there must be some, somewhere! But just what are the odds? How do we calculate it?

Way back in the mid-20th century, an astrophysicist named Frank Drake tried to come up with a mathematical model in order to determine just that. This so-called "Drake Equation" theoretically could be used to estimate just how many alien civilizations might be in the galaxy that we'd possibly be able to communicate with. There were a number of factors and ratios that were all multiplied by each other to come up with a solution.

Unfortunately, every single variable at the time was a complete guess. Over Dr. Drake's lifetime, though, a lot of those figures became able to be numerated (or at least, the estimates became closer to plausibly true). For instance, we had a reasonable idea of the rate of star formation in the galaxy, and by the early 21st century we were quite sure that every single star had planets around it, even some in their habitable zones—the area around a sun where the planet's distance could potentially allow liquid water to exist on the surface. At that time, things were looking quite bright. As the 21st and 22nd centuries unfolded, we were able to find many Earth-sized rocky worlds in their sun's habitable zones. Estimates put the number of alien civilizations in the millions!

However, during that same timeframe, it became very clear that we needed to make some adjustments to this equation. Originally, one factor determined if a planet could support life and it was multiplied by another element that ascertained if life would actually form. These two components, nevertheless, did not go deep enough, and we had a pretty good idea why that was. Many more specifics needed to be taken into account.

Well before humankind even left the Sol System, it was quite clear that life was much more precarious than was hoped. After spending vast spans of time searching rocky bodies like Mars;

watery moons like Europa, Enceladus, Calisto, Ganymede, and more; and even planetoids with atmospheres similar to Earth's like Saturn's moon Titan—no signs of life, past or present, were ever found. Even the idea of how big the "habitable zone" should be had to be shrunk into a tighter circle.

Conversely, it wasn't just the lack of finding life, but the inability to spread life even in our own solar system. There were massive expectations, but humans were simply unable to terraform Mars and turn it into a second home. Nonetheless, these unsuccessful efforts provided useful data in the search for worlds that humans could potentially settle on later.

Core among the learned requirements was the need for a naturally strong magnetic field to protect any atmosphere and the surface from deadly cosmic radiation. In order to have an active magnetic field, during early solar system formation, a planet would need to be hit by another body that was almost equal in size and the two would have to merge together. This would give it an oversized molten core that could spin and still provide warmth to the surface. Mars's interior had, for the most part, seized up billions of years in the past. This also led to a lack of tectonic activity—the literal process of the surface crust being recycled, continents drifting across the globe, and mountains being built as the landmasses collided into each other—another seemingly significant factor to having and maintaining life.

These were not the only knocks against the red planet. Many people tried to brush off its small size—resulting in the pull of gravity being around one-third that of Earth—as no major concern. However, that singular component of Martian existence made it so that humans and all the other living things they brought with them had a plethora of health issues. In the end, the colonists were forced to live underground in artificially lit tunnels. But calling it "living" is a stretch of the definition of the word as their lifespans were cut severely short compared to their contemporaries back on Earth.

There was a thought for a while that the lessons learned on Mars could be applied to Venus. Afterall, Venus is roughly 90% of Earth's size and gravity, really the blue marble's twin in many ways. Unfortunately, that did not work out either. It would take a totally different approach to figure out how humans could create useful environments without causing unnecessary mass destruction.

That came once scientists were able to take control of asteroids in the Belt and hollow them out. After that, they would spin them up so the centrifugal force would simulate 1G on the inside with people living on the outward edges. They actually found this to be a much more successful method for creating a habitable ecosystem, so Mars and the rest of the heavenly bodies were basically abandoned. Yes, millions of people still survive today spread out among these rocky and wet worlds, but none could be considered thriving.

More importantly, from all of these failures we gleaned the knowledge of what to look for in exoplanets. Even an Earth-analogue around a G-type star is not a good choice for a colony if the chemical makeup and mix is too far off the mark from what we have on Earth. All of that needs to be nearly perfect for terraforming efforts to take and stick. Still, everything from the atmosphere downwards has to be manually maintained by a dedicated crew. That said, each new colony brings us one step closer to understanding how life may emerge innately without intervention.

Which brings us back to the Drake Equation. These are but a few among the many aspects we think are important for understanding the formation of life as we know it. Depending upon how one plugs in the assumptions, it is possible to end up with just one civilization forming in an entire galaxy. Yes, we could potentially be alone in the Milky Way. The good news is that there are billions of galaxies out there that we have yet to explore!

"Salutations, space-cadets, this is episode number one-forty-seven of <u>Quantum Dish</u>, all is nominal, and I am your host: Beth Oh," said our self-named host of the podcast. "If this is y'all's first time tuning in, every week we are joined by a very special guest to parse through the hottest news, rumors, and gossip from the deep, cold reaches of outer space! And listeners, we are closing in on epic episode number one-fifty, so be sure y'all are subscribed, spread the word, and mash that like-button on your favorite podcast provider. And if you would care to support me directly, be sure to follow the link in the episode description so I can continue to bring you great content like this every week!

"Now, we have an exceptionally wonderful guest for y'all today! Joining me for this hour is one of the biggest names in morning news. Please welcome to the mic, Jaimé Ayuda!"

"Thanks for having me, Beth," Jaimé chimed

in by way of introduction.

Beth's chipper voice quickly responded, "No, thank you for coming into the studio. I understand you have a new project you've been working on that our listeners are sure to love, coming out in just two weeks?"

Jaimé went on to describe some limited programming that actually seemed rather unrelated to the general theme of the podcast. This went on for quite a while, followed by a commercial break for some sponsors. Finally, the host and guest returned to what was the main impetus of this program; namely, hearsay around interstellar travel.

"Okay, Jaimé," Beth proclaimed, "let's talk about Marco Chung! What's the dish? Give me the juicy details!"

Jaimé laughed and asked, "What do you want to know? I'll tell you what I've heard."

"First off, where is he?" Beth queried. "He doesn't have a home anywhere on Earth and he can't even go up the space elevator until a year has passed, so he must be somewhere planetside. Where's he staying? I mean, don't give me an address or anything, but around where can he be found? No one's even seen him since his appearance on your co-host Veronica Dubois's afternoon talk show."

"Whoa, whoa, whoa, slow down, Beth," chided Jaimé. "Despite being more revealing than usual during Veronica's show, Marco is known to be intensely private, avoiding the limelight as he's become more renown. My friends have told me that after his experience on Veronica's show, he'd rather go back into hiding and return to a life of supposed anonymity. I mean, good luck with that, but basically, he's been squatting at some out-of-sight beach rental."

"So, you do know where he is?" Beth pleaded.

"Well," Jaimé demurred, "I have a good idea of where he could be, but it'd be no use. He's not in a mood to see or talk to anyone in the media anymore, myself included."

"Awwww, that stinks," Beth whined.

Jaimé tried to assuage her sadness saying, "Well, he's not completely alone."

"Wait, wait!" exclaimed Beth, "Is Veronica there with him?"

"What?!" Jaimé seemed completely taken aback by this line of questioning. "Why would you think Veronica would be with him?"

One could almost hear Beth blushing over the airwaves. "Well, Veronica really gushes over him, and she somehow got an exclusive interview that no one else has ever been able to land. Their relationship seems a little more... intimate."

"¡Ay dios mio..." Jaimé trailed off.

"Do you deny it?" accused Beth. "I mean, you are Veronica's co-host, you see her almost every day, so no one would know more about this situation than you."

"Where do you get such ideas?" Jaimé deflected.

"It's all over the boards!" Beth claimed, defensively.

"Oh, I know I'm going to regret this," Jaimé began, "but let me squash some rumors right now. There is a reason I know the things I do, and it has nothing—I repeat: nothing—to do with dear Veronica.

"Go on..." Beth prompted.

"Here's the deal," Jaimé went on, "there have been some interceptions of communiques that we can confirm have come to and from Marco.

It's all hush hush, highly encrypted stuff. From what we've been able to glean from some of the less careful correspondents, he may even have had some guests."

"Some guests, you say?" perked up Beth. "Would one of those callers happen to be a certain lady whose name rhymes with harmonica?"

"Give it a rest, Beth!" an exasperated Jaimé demanded, although it was unclear if he was upset with the path the queries were taking or with the constant mentions of Veronica.

"Okay, okay," Beth gave in, "but why all the secrecy?"

"Who knows?" Jaimé admitted. "The man has been in HSA for centuries; he might just be accustomed to their protocols and does everything ultra-secure."

"Do you think he could be talking to HSA about his next mission?" Beth hypothesized.

"I, actually, wouldn't count on Marco Chung being on any future mission," Jaimé offered.

Beth let out a loud gasp, followed by a short scream. "What do you mean? On Veronica's show, he said he was going to go out there if he had his way. I even heard him tell autograph seekers after the taping that he had some sort of 'grand finale' of sorts planned. They asked him for details, but per usual he was tight lipped."

"Well, consider this an exclusive," offered Jaimé. "I have it on good authority from sources within HSA that Marco is going to retire, whether he wants to or not."

"No way!"

"Yes way! Do you realize what an insane amount of money HSA will have to pay him if he goes out there again? Listen, they love him, but they still have to think about the economics of the situation. Marco Chung is only one pilot, and they have others. There is also another problem: there is a growing handful of people that have been inspired by Marco and want to go on many more trips. At first, HSA was thrilled to get experienced crewmembers coming back for second, third, and even fourth journeys. But more tours of duty than that, and having several people doing it at once… they just can't afford to keep it up. They need to cut costs to stay solvent."

"Wow," sighed Beth, "it could really all just come down to money? They would end one of the most storied space travel careers in history over something like that?"

"It's not just that," Jaimé offered. "The man is a hundred-sixty-whatever of his own years old and looks the worse-for-wear. He not only got the life extending treatments too late to take advantage of their full benefits, but he has also been absorbing cosmic radiation forever. Despite all of our advances in healthcare, you can't just overcome all of that compounded cellular damage."

"Given all those rads," interrupted Beth, "how come he's not dying of cancer right now?"

Jaimé countered, "How do we know he isn't? He doesn't exactly post his personal info all over social media. All this talk of big plans he has, perhaps part of that is dying on the job? And that is a liability that HSA just does not want. He'd be more useful as a recruiter, spokesperson, and figurehead on Earth than as a potential hazard out among the stars."

"So," considered Beth, "HSA would rather have him announce his own retirement and give him a cush gig than risk sending him on another mission?"

"Yes... but no, it's bigger than that," Jaimé

retorted. "They would rather Marco retire himself than be made to look like jerks by firing him. The whole Human Expansion Program is dependent upon their sparkling reputation. HSA is a government-sponsored monopoly that must remain squeaky clean in order to have the trust of the people."

"Makes sense," Beth acquiesced. "Sadly, I get it. It does make you wonder, though, why Marco is so hellbent on getting out there? What more could he possibly have to prove? And what does he have planned for this 'grand finale' of his?"

"There's only one thing it could be," Jaimé teased.

"What's that?"

"Life."

"Do you think Marco knows where to find life beyond Earth, and wants to be the one to officially discover it?" Beth posited.

"If you are asking if he knows for sure," Jaimé began, "then the answer is no. If you are asking if he doesn't want to walk off this mortal coil without finding at least an alien microbe, then that would absolutely be it. Why else would he keep subjecting himself to all of this? Even Marco

Chung has to be feeling old and beat up and wanting to move on. But how can he do it without completing, as he called it, his 'duty'?"

"You make a good point," Beth granted. "But we've been most everywhere worthwhile in the galaxy and have yet to find any evidence of modern or primordial life."

Turning the interview around, Jaimé asked, "Do you believe there is life out there?"

"Of course!" Beth quickly retorted. "There has to be, probability tells us so."

"Then where is it?" Jaimé pestered.

"What are you, a Sixth Dayer now?" Beth snapped back.

"Now, now," Jaimé offered in a calming voice, "no need for name calling. I'm just proposing a hypothetical for you."

"I mean," Beth stumbled, "it might just be that it is exceedingly rare. Maybe it only happens once in a galaxy, or once in every ten galaxies!"

"And there you go," Jaimé jeered.

"Hold on, hold on, hold on," Beth demanded, pumping the brakes. "Are you saying that Marco wants to leave the galaxy? That's impossible!"

"Impossible right now," corrected Jaimé.

"There are no limits to performing a Quantum Shift aside from observational technologies—we have to know where we are going in order to get there—and the computational power to make it happen. Given enough data and time, even if that epoch is in the far future, we should be able to shift that distance."

"Still, a whole other galaxy, a new frontier?" Beth doubted. "Honestly, we still struggle getting around within the Milky Way right now."

"Consider this," Jaimé offered. "The Canis Major Dwarf Galaxy is only 25,000 light-years away. The Milky Way is around 100,000 light-years wide. In other words, the outskirts of the Canis Major Dwarf Galaxy are closer to us than parts of the Milky Way we've already been to and/or colonized."

"Hmmm... you do make a compelling argument," Beth accepted. "Well, that gives us a lot of food for thought. Let's talk about that and more, right after this word from today's sponsors. We'll be right back!"

RECORD #12: SEEDS

<u>FOR IMMEDIATE RELEASE</u>

The Human Space Agency (HSA) is proud to announce a major breakthrough in Quantum Drive technology. Using recently developed observational techniques, parallel quantum computing processing power, and expanded artificial intelligence algorithms—beginning with the next generation of Quantum Ships that are launching later this year, it will now be possible to travel to nearby galaxies in the local group.

While discussing this exciting news during an earlier press conference, Director of the Human Space Agency David Clarke proclaimed, "These accomplishments to expand the capabilities of the Quantum Drive system have been decades in the making. I would like to thank all of our dedicated, highly skilled team-members who were working on this project, even if they did not know they were a part of it. Due to the strict laws and overarching policies of the Terran government, information on the operations of Quantum Drives must remain highly compartmentalized, even within HSA itself. Despite this challenging environment, our people persevered in order to overcome the seemingly impossible."

More so, the scientific leaps that have been made are retroactively compatible. Because of this, and the unique scheduling situation that led to all Quantum Ships being available in the Sol System at the same time, right now every single one is being retrofitted with the necessary components so that they, too, can later head out to other galaxies. All of the ships were already going through routine maintenance and other upgrades, so—as long as hiring goals remain on pace—there is no expectation that these latest additions will delay their next missions.

Currently, the new methodology is limited to an area within 100,000 light-years. That theoretically still means there are about ten neighboring galaxies that are potential landing spots. While all of these are relatively small compared to our own Milky Way, they are actually being treated more as dropping off points. The anticipated plan at this time is to only launch mapping missions that will provide data for another 100,000 light-years out. With that data, and repeating the process over-and-over again, it will become possible to expand the field of vision and information outward so that we can Quantum Shift further and further away and partake in proper exploration and colonization. The originally planned schedule for the entire fleet over the next several decades is being revamped as we speak in order to accommodate this imperative exploration phase.

Summarizing these developments, Director Clarke went on to tell the assembled media, "With all that we have announced today, we'll finally be able to spread the seeds of humanity to the rest of the universe. And, per our mission statement, as we propagate the stars, we ensure that humanity will be able to live forever!"

Record #13: Backup

During our interview, Marco Chung told me, "We used to call it 'Plan B' for short because it was the nearest Earth-sized world in its star's habitable zone. When I was a kid, we absolutely thought it was the best backup option for humanity in case something went horribly wrong with the Earth and/or the Sol System. Despite its well-known shortcomings, compared to the other choices, it felt fairly handy. Of course, having made that journey several times, I can tell you it is still a very long ride."

Marco was speaking about Proxima Centauri B, a rocky world orbiting the star Proxima Centauri, which is "only" about 4.3 light-years from Earth. Due to its relative proximity (Get it? "Proxima" literally translates to "nearest". No one ever said astronomers were that creative!) and size, Plan B became the focus of the nascent extrasolar exploration and settlement industry. Once the energy barrier for Torch Drives was overcome, the first long-term mission was sent to Proxima Centauri to assess the possibility of setting up a permanent colony in the system. Probes had been sent there as far back as the late 21st century using archaic techniques like a laser pushing a lightweight sensor, but nothing we have built has ever beat a pair of human eyes.

Proxima Centauri itself is unlike anything we experience in the Sol System. First off, it is part of a trinary cluster named Alpha Centauri whose three stars all rotate around each other. The other two stars—Rigil Kentaurus and Toliman—are both sort of Sol-like, but far enough off that they no longer are considered that similar to Earth's sun. They are so close to each other that for a long while astronomers thought they were just one star! If we pretend that one of them was Sol, their eccentric orbits around each other would place the other one at a distance between Pluto-Charon and Saturn. Can you imagine having another sun where Uranus is and what that would do to planetary formation?

The answer is, nothing good. Even if we considered those stars to be better options for a possible colony (we don't, but more on that later), there is not an Earth-analogue to be found in their habitable zones, at least not stably. Which brings us back to Proxima Centauri. It actually orbits almost like a planet around the other two stars at a distance equivalent to Neptune. This has given the bodies that orbit it much more steadiness than could possibly be achieved around its siblings.

Unlike the other two, Proxima Centauri is a red dwarf, a much smaller, lighter, and cooler star compared to yellow dwarfs like Sol. We won't get into the definition of different types of stars (I have another book on that subject you can read, if you're interested), but basically, the bigger and hotter a star, the faster it burns through its fuel and dies—often violently. And although we call them both dwarfs, the red ones are around 8% to 50% the mass of the yellow bunch. That all said, there is something more important than size, especially at the smaller end of that scale. The key to a red dwarf's desirability is its lifespan.

Sol will finish burning through its hydrogen in about 5 billion years. Of course, we don't have to worry about that because the Earth will be burnt to a crisp in just a billion years as the sun expands, unless we can somehow move the planet out of the way. On the other hand, Proxima Centauri will take 4 _trillion_ years to reach a similar milestone. We'll put aside its own phases and changes for now—the important thing is that red dwarfs last a very, very long time, and we like that so we don't have to move very often.

And the good news keeps rolling in because red dwarfs make up something like 70% of the stars in the observable universe. Then, on top of that, something like 90% of them have rocky, Earth-size-ish worlds. This is the dream come true: nearly unlimited places we can colonize and spread humanity!

As you have undoubtedly noticed by the limited number of colonies we have been able to prop up, there is a problem. Because Proxima Centauri is so much cooler than Sol, its habitable zone is also that much closer to it. How intimate is the star with its planets? Well, a year on Plan B is just 11.2 Earth-days. And we use the term "year" very loosely here because Plan B is tidally locked with its sun. In other words, one side always faces Proxima Centauri and is an inhospitable, burning desert where the red sun never sets. The other side is a frozen wasteland where the concept of a warm ball in the sky is completely unheard of.

In the middle, though, along what we might call the meridian—an imaginary line going north/south around a globe, like the opposite of an equator—is a "temperate" zone. There, the sun is at an angle where we might consider it rising or setting, except it will never move and will instead just stay at the same position on the horizon all the time. Yes, a red orb in the sky that never moves and keeps the area in a perpetual dawn/dusk. Whoever had a monopoly on sleeping masks and blackout curtains would be guaranteed to make a fortune!

Nevertheless, that oblique angle is perfectly able to keep it just warm enough that liquid water could exist on the surface, given an appropriate local atmosphere and pressure.

When we arrived at Plan B, we did not find any pre-existing atmosphere and the water was basically trapped on the dark side of the planet in glaciers the size of continents. However, we did see that the meridian was surrounded by mountains of rock on the sun-side and ice on the dark-side. As such, in our hubris, we thought we could create an atmosphere just in that little strip of land that would keep the valley safe for all life—although no life had ever formed there of its own volition.

At first, things looked good. But then the sun flared and destroyed the meager bits of atmosphere we had managed to get going. Again and again, by the actual definition of insanity, we thought we could overcome the very nature of the cosmic arrangement. Finally, we came to accept the hard reality: we could never live on the surface of Plan B or any planet like it. Red dwarfs were not ever going to be a viable option.

Of course, a colony still exists on Plan B to this day, but it is underground and no better than living on the underside of any rocky body anywhere in the galaxy, especially options much closer to home. Because humans generally crave being able to walk around freely outside, Plan B remains a minor outpost of just a few hundred thousand people. Sadly, this situation is not even the worst thing Plan B's inhabitants have to deal with.

I claimed that Plan B is an Earth-like world, but that was another one of my little tricky exaggerations. Back then they thought it was an Earth-analogue because it was a rocky world in a habitable zone that was somewhat Earth's size. But there was a big caveat in that "somewhat" that we now understand to be critical. With a measured gravity that makes things weigh on average about 14% differently than on Earth, this discrepancy in downward force is destructive to life. The lifespans of the natives of Plan B (humans, animals, plants, bacteria, whatever) are significantly less than those on Earth and other later colonies. Gravity sickness is very real, and we need to be in a much more specific range to thrive, something like 0.98G to 1.02G.

The devastation of losing hope in Plan B was immediate. Proposals to go to places like Trappist were completely scrapped. Even though Trappist is nearly 41 light-years away, it boasts several Earth-sized worlds in its habitable zone—including ones that would fit our modern definition of an Earth-analogue. Plan B was considered the jumping off point before heading to Trappist to create several new worlds in one system.

However, because of the unfortunate experiences at Proxima Centauri B, the entire Human Expansion Program had to be discarded and rebuilt from scratch.

RECORD #14: WHEN

MORNING SHOW SEGMENT

"And now, it's time for <u>Today, Last Year!</u>" exclaimed the deep-throated announcer after the opening teaser had rolled.

"Thank you, Larry, as always, for such a stirring introduction!" Veronica Dubois said to the disembodied voice, "And hello again to all of you at home. And, of course, salutations to you, my indispensable co-host Jaimé Ayuda. Why don't you let everyone know what we have in store for this hour?"

"My pleasure, Veronica," Jaimé responded back with about as much gusto as he could muster. "In case this is your first time, <u>Today, Last Year!</u> is a segment where we sift through all of the data that has come in from the extrasolar colonies and bring you the biggest stories, no matter how long ago they really happened."

"That's right," Veronica chimed in with practiced professionalism. "Even though we can travel anywhere instantly with the Quantum

Drive, the rules of the universe still apply. That means that the speed of light is as fast as communication can go."

"Well, Veronica," Jaimé interrupted in what did not appear to be a part of their rehearsed routine, "it actually goes a bit slower than that. Data jumps between repeaters and boosters so we do not have signal degradation."

Veronica quickly recovered from Jaimé seemingly going off script and responded, "Yes, well, if we really were using those traditional methods, it would take about four and half years to get a message even from nearby Proxima Centauri. But, as you know Jaimé, with humanity spread further and further outward across the galaxy, it has become impractical to use radio-waves as our primary communication method. Who is going to wait 80,000 years for the latest news from Novissimus?"

"Absolutely no one," agreed Jaimé. "Instead, we just download the entire local internet from a colony and bring it back with us on a Quantum Ship as if it were another piece of cargo. That cuts the time down to just under an eight-year delay, much better!"

Veronica chuckled in a way she must have done the same way countless times before. "True, Jaimé, although even far away colonies still send out their data through the traditional methodologies as a redundant backup. Sadly, Proxima Centauri is the only one close enough where this technique is actually faster!"

"If only anything interesting ever happened on Plan B," Jaimé let slip.

Veronica's veneer fell for a moment as she shot Jaimé a death glare. Nevertheless, it was quite a brief interlude before she was able to reestablish her smile and sparkle. With those back in place, Veronica said "Even then, it's still more efficient to upload and download the data than it is to send it out."

"Of course, of course," Jaimé acquiesced. "But no matter the source, there's still a lot of data to parse through. It takes some time to find out what is newsworthy..."

"... and what is just pictures of baby animals!" Veronica said finishing Jaimé's sentence. They both had a good laugh at this as it was apparently a part of their routine for Veronica to fill in the blank with whatever the frivolous token was to be used as a comparison. "So, Jaimé, what is your newest discovery?"

"Oh, Veronica, you, especially, are going to find this one quite interesting."

"Do tell!" Veronica implored.

"Well, speaking of far off Novissimus," Jaimé began, "I've got one that has gotten back to us in far less than 80,000 years."

"Novissimus, you say?" a flummoxed and stumbling Veronica said with a twang of apprehension in her voice.

"Yes, exactly," Jaimé stated, taking back the reins. "Apparently, while planet-side during the most recent mission, one of the high-ranking crew members got into a bar fight with some local riffraff."

Jaimé paused and waited for Veronica's response. Finally, she flatly asked, "Which one?"

Jaimé's smile practically expanded beyond his face as he answered, "Amazingly, it was none other than the captain of the Quantum Ship and the entire mission, and the oldest man in the universe: Marco Chung!"

Seemingly knowing that she could not get out of this, Veronica dove deeper by querying, "Do you know what led up to this alleged so-called altercation?"

"That I do!" Jaimé declared. "From video taken by a bystander, we can see that several patrons were bugging Captain Chung about how they could join the crew and be a part of a mission themselves."

While watching clips of the prepared video roll, Veronica proposed, "That all looks and sounds rather benign."

"Yes, but as we are about to see, Marco actually tries to dissuade them. Veronica, why wouldn't Marco want to recruit more people? HSA always needs additional able-bodied personnel who are willing to partake in and work on the long journeys."

"I could only speculate..." Veronica trailed off by way of a response.

"Please do," Jaimé requested. "I'd be really interested in knowing your perspective on this."

"Well, I think I need more context," Veronica deflected. "What did they say to Marco? Did Marco express anything back?"

"Unfortunately," Jaimé admitted, "the audio is not that great with all of the noise of the bar and the music and such. All I know for certain is that they took great offense to Marco trying to convince them not to join up. Someone who indicated that they were there wrote in the comments that they heard Marco say something along the lines of 'those folks would be a plague upon the cosmos.'"

"Well, there you have it, Jaimé," Veronica confidently asserted. "I guess those guys must have been real jerks. I'd trust Marco Chung's judgement any day on who should and shouldn't be out there!"

RECORD #15: PETITION
SNIPPET FROM A LIVE STREAM

The avatar for FasterThanMach69 appeared on the screen, apparently a surprise guest at hour number six of the live stream. While everyone else had arrived as a real-life person until this point, it appeared that Mach preferred to preserve his particular level of anonymity—or perhaps wanted to maintain his façade and the distance his representative illustration gave him.

"Hello my celestial friends," Mach began by way of his usual greeting, although his avatar's mouth was not moving. "No, this isn't a special live episode of <u>Cosmological Quandaries</u>, but it is nonetheless a special cause. Usually, I try to stay away from the politics of outer space and just attempt to report on the facts in a way that makes them fun, easy, and—hopefully—entertaining. However, something has come to my attention that I felt I just had to speak up about."

Mach's avatar moved over to the right side of the screen from the viewer's perspective and a cutout of Marco Chung with a wooden stick attached to his bottom slid in from the watcher's left. Mach continued, "Everyone, this is a personal inspiration of mine and someone I'm quite sure you're all familiar with, especially from all the airtime I've given him over the years discussing his life and work. Please, let me introduce the definition of vintage itself, Captain Marco Chung of the HSA Quantum Fleet!"

"Hello there, Mach," a poor impersonation of Marco Chung's voice that was obviously really Mach said. "You are an inspiration to me, too!"

"Oh, thank you so much, Captain Chung," Mach said with all the false humility he could muster—which is to say, none.

"Please, I like to think that we are close friends," the Captain Chung puppet said, "Call me Marco, or, you know, something more familiar, like buddy!"

"You got it, buddy!" Mach said as his avatar finally moved to give two thumbs-up. "But do you know what we're doing here today?"

"I want to go to spaaaaaaaaaaacccccccceeeeee!" Mach's buddy screamed.

"And me and everyone here wants you to be

able to go," Mach conceded. "For some reason, though, there's a problem. We're just a few months away from when the majority of the Quantum Fleet is supposed to leave on their new missions and you have not been assigned a ship yet. More so, HSA has continually refused to comment on your status and if they are going to let you sign up or not."

"Whaaaaaa!" the puppet cried as it started raining tears in the background.

"I know, I know," Mach said as his avatar moved in for something akin to a pat on the back. "It's not right, not right at all. You know, though, that's why me and my friends all came together. We're going to get you a posting no matter what!"

"How are you going to do that?" the popsicle-stick-based depiction inquired with a sniffle.

"Well, buddy, what you are seeing is what we are doing about it," began Mach's explanation. "We're doing this live stream to get everyone to sign a petition and force HSA to come clean and give you an assignment. Everyone here right now, those watching on Earth and Luna live, and even people in the Sol System colonies on ever-increasing delays believe in you and are on board to sign the petition to get you aboard!"

"It's currently about five light-hours from Earth to Pluto-Charon," offered Marco's likeness on a stick.

"Yes," agreed Mach, "and that demonstration of knowledge is another reason why you belong out there. We are not going to stop streaming until 100 million individuals sign the petition!"

"How many people have signed it so far?" asked Marco's proxy.

"Well, let's see here..." Mach trailed off as he supposedly went to check some figures. "Eh... it looks like about 12 million. Oh boy, it's going to be a long night!"

RECORD #16: BELIEF

INTERNAL MEMO

TO: High Priest Council

RE: Status on Recruitment of Marco Chung

Your Excellencies,

As per your request, I have prepared the below summary report on all of our efforts to date into the conversion of Captain Marco Chung of the HSA Quantum Ship Fleet into the Lord's light under the auspices of the Holy Church of the Sixth Day Reclamation. Being Chief Missionary, I wish to personally assuage your concerns and reiterate from our prior discussion that we have been dedicating all available and reasonable resources to this undertaking. You can rest assured that we in the Missionary Division share the same goals as what you laid out and that we have acted with the utmost seriousness and devotion that this task deserves. With God's divine guidance, we shall soon finally bear fruit.

In order to fully comprehend where we

currently stand, it is important to also know how this all began. Around 25 years ago, a junior missionary took it upon herself to approach Marco Chung after he had returned from his 13th blasphemous journey, the 8th using the devil's quantum toolkit. While it would normally seem that the very symbol of the evil we oppose could not be brought around to see the Lord's grace and wisdom, God appeared to have steered this young woman into a unique confluence of circumstances.

This particular operation was apparently a complete failure that resulted in a colony collapse, as is want to happen when the unfaithful ignore God's will. However, that level of disappointment seemed to have left Marco Chung feeling vulnerable, questioning his very purpose. In that moment, he became open to the truth for the first time.

We must not think too harshly about Marco Chung despite all that he has done against the will of God. Marco was born into unjust conditions and in a world before the reclamation; he never had the opportunity to learn about the blessed one's wisdom, decrees, and laws. He knew naught of the holy texts nor the guidance and peace that can be found in God's embrace. He is, perhaps, the most lost soul of all. Is it not our ordained duty to save his restless spirit, and in the process, rescue all of the Almighty's glorious creation?

But because he has been under the nameless one's hold for so long, it has taken our missionaries many visits to unravel these knots and start to set him free to walk with the Lord. During that first encounter, he was willing to listen, and the young lady was allowed to visit him on several more occasions to further educate him. Ultimately, she was unable to fully release him from Satan's grip, and Marco Chung opted to leave the cradle of life again.

This would be the same pattern upon his next return. My predecessor took some more... radical actions that I did not approve of when I was his subordinate. While Marco Chung was on Earth, he sent many more missionaries Marco's way, all who reported that Marco was still willing to listen and asked questions, but they appeared no closer to bringing him fully around. Because of this, an even more extreme action was taken.

Missionaries were placed on all outbound Quantum Ships. Their purpose was three-fold. First, they were to use their time aboard to convince passengers not to become sinners by turning into colonists. Our missionaries were to reiterated that it was not too late for them, that they could choose to not disembark at their vile destination planet, and that they could promptly return to God's one gift for all life without penalty. Second, and most controversially, some were to remain in the pits of hell in order to help save souls and convince these lost sheep to abandon their slovenly ways and return to Earth. And finally, some of them were bound to be on the same vessel as Marco Chung. With this, they would have had unfettered access to the Captain for years on end.

While the decision to send any of God's creatures out of his one true creation was surely a transgression against his will—and the man who formerly held my position was deservedly defrocked for doing so—it is hard to ignore the results. Upon returning from the heavens, Marco Chung's mind appeared ready for revelations. It was at that point that I personally took over his case, and have been his main point of contact and confidant for eight years now. Much to my eternal shame, I was unable to dissuade him from his most recent commission, but he was able to bring tidings from our lost brothers and sisters stuck in the abyss known as "Novissimus". They are in poor condition due to being separated from God's eternal flame and are ready to return home. Captain Chung has given them comforts that they will soon be able to do so, though I know not by what means.

To clarify, I am well aware of statements Marco Chung has made to news sites about desiring to blast off from Earth's hold again, as well as rumors of HSA attempting to force him into retirement. Either of these situations would be detrimental to our cause. I, too, consider Marco Chung the top priority target for spreading God's message. Having Marco Chung renounce the Human Expansion Program would be the most important piece of propaganda the Church could ever ask for. However, if that came after he was involuntarily separated from his duties, it would look like "sour grapes", to use a colloquialism, and the message would be lost.

I know I am asking for a lot, but patience is

the most important thing here. We must let Marco work through the process himself and come to the light in his own way. That may mean allowing him to once again commit the most horrific offence so that we can forgive him later, just as undoubtedly God will absolve Marco for all of his lapses in moral turpitude. However, I do not think it will come to this as I have arrived at the belief that Marco's desire to be placed on one more mission is nothing but a ruse.

Although I did not reveal the extent of the Missionary Division's involvement with Marco Chung before our meeting, it was never my intention to deceive or mislead any member of the Council. I was just using the resources we have been allocated to undertake our most virtuous of duties in the manner I best saw fit. Before this time, Marco Chung had never asked anything of me, any other missionary, or the Church in general. When he requested our help to accomplish this undertaking, I leapt at the rare opportunity to provide something for Marco to further build out our trust and understanding.

Yes, I admit that I do not fully comprehend what we have been tasked to do, nor what it will accomplish. It is all very technical and beyond my level of understanding. All I know for certain is that Marco has guaranteed me that no one will be harmed by what he has prepared and that it will be the catalyst the Church so desperately wants and needs.

Although it is difficult to accept, this is the path to having Marco Chung officially and openly join our flock. We must have faith, as we have always preached, and give Marco all of the personnel and resources necessary to complete this enterprise. Marco has also been very generous with us, providing all the funding necessary and even more for other areas of our calling. I do not need to ask; he has just been willing to provide. I know of no other way to explain that Marco is truly a part of the Holy Church of the Sixth Day Reclamation in all but an official declaration, but is just waiting for the most impactful moment to make that announcement to the rest of creation.

What we must do, then, is provide what he has asked for, especially since he is willing to pay for all of it. There is no risk to the Church, its leadership, or its members, so please do not bring all our exertions to a premature end; not after all we have been able to accomplish thus far. Instead, now is the critical moment to redouble our labors, for time is of the essence.

Record #17: Requirements

Thus, the "better worlds initiative" was launched in order to find just that: worthier planets that humans could colonize, terraform, and safely live on the surface. But how to narrow it down and find such a place? Well, eliminating red dwarfs from the equation takes 70% of the possible destinations right off the table. On the other end, stars larger than Sol have a habit of prematurely blowing up as supernovae. Even when we did surveys of stars like these, we generally did not find rocky Earth-ish size planets in their habitable zones. As such, we said, "Hey, if we want things that are a good fit for us, let's just stick with stars like our own sun!"

Our sun's size, luminosity, and elemental makeup puts it in a class of stars known as G-type. When we look out into the galaxy, we can see that about 7% of stars in the Milky Way fall into this category. Again, far less than red dwarfs, but not insignificant. There are something like 400 billion stars in the Milky Way alone, so that would leave about 28 billion as potential new homes—certainly nothing to sneeze at. Every human could have their own planet with plenty to spare!

Unfortunately, classifications like G-type are completely artificial and mean nothing. There is actually quite a wide range of differences between all of these ostensibly similar yellow dwarfs. Once we factor in circumference (how wide it is around), density (how packed together it is on the inside), metallicity (the abundance of elements other than hydrogen and helium), and similar contributing factors, we cut the rate down to about 2% of stars—something like 8 billion. Sadly, now a bunch of people will have to share their planet with another person!

Oh, wait, that would require all of those stars to have planets that we could put to use. And although they all have orbiting bodies of one kind or another, they are not all useful. Take Tau Ceti for instance. It's a Sol-analogue just 12 light-years from Earth with a bunch of rocky worlds in its habitable zone. But all of those planets are so-called "Super Earths", terrestrial orbs that are between the mass of one and a half to ten Earths. Any bigger than that and a planet starts to become an ice giant like Uranus or Neptune. As we have shown with Plan B and other experiences dealing with gravity, even a little difference is too much for us in the long term. A lot more disparity will just crush us, anyway.

Let's recap, then, what we are looking for in an Earth-analogue. It needs a size and density close to Earth with around 1G of gravity; an oversized molten core from a collision with a similarly massed planetoid in the distant past that resulted in a strong magnetic field plus active plate tectonics; having a somewhat-but-not-too-great elliptical orbit that stays within a much-reduced habitable zone; and containing the correct ratio of various elements and compounds that are accessible within a few meters of the surface. However, as the infomercials say, "But, wait, there's more!"

The planet also should have a tilt so that there are seasons, and that tilt needs to be somewhere between 20-25 degrees and be relatively stable. How do we get it to be stable? Well, we need a natural satellite, a.k.a. a moon! But not just any moon will do. It must be like Earth's moon Luna where it is 1-2% of the host planet's mass, but much less dense (or as I like to say, fluffier). For example, Luna is 1.2% of Earth's mass, but is 25% of its diameter. Think of Earth as a hard cheese that has been left out of the refrigerator for too long and has taken on puck-like properties while Luna is a spreadable margarine. The moon isn't made of cheese; it's made out of whipped butter!

But a moon like that—which must also be an acceptable distance away from the planet—helps keep the tilt steady, which in turn maintains the seasons. On top of that, an object of that size creates the tides as parts of the planet bulges towards its current location in its orbit, attracted by its gravity. Yet, that is also why it must be just one moon. Having multiple objects in the sky creates competing forces that cannot be overcome. We learned that the hard way, too.

Okay, with all of these requirements, we have now cut our pool down to a fraction of a fraction of a fraction of a percent. If we wanted to live underground or in spinning asteroids, there would be plenty of options. Realistically, though, the whole point is to either find life or plant it there through terraforming so that we can freely walk on the surface as if it were our home-world. That said, what do we specifically mean by "life", and what is "terraforming" if we don't find it?

Well, both are quite difficult questions to answer. We think that "life" is when certain chemical compounds come together and start to intake a catalyst in order to self-replicate in an organized and intentional manner. How do we make the jump from being just a bunch of chemicals to a living organism? Regrettably, even though we understand all of the constituent parts, we have never been able to convince new life to emerge in a laboratory setting. Sure, we can modify existing life by manipulating its DNA and RNA, but we still cannot seem to just build RNA and force it to create a container around itself. There is something we are missing.

Since our understanding is that RNA came first and DNA evolved later, we are generally on the lookout for it. Even on bodies in the Sol System, we can find plenty of what we claim are "organic molecules", the compounds that make up the sugars we see in RNA, DNA, and similar entities that we consider crucial for life. We are also aware of other molecules with the same shapes as seen in the RNA and/or DNA of all life on Earth, so we keep an eye peeled for those, too. And to be clear, we do find plenty of every type of organic molecule wherever we go.

However, at no point outside of Earth have we found a place where any of those molecules have spontaneously come together to form life. But since those chemical chains do exist, we can put them to use for our purposes. With the right makeup and mix of elements and compounds, we can instead try to coax our own Earthly life to take root. This is the process we call "terraforming". On a global scale, we ensure the existence of critical components like an ozone layer, an air mixture, and a proper pressure. In the ground we build soil and carefully introduce genetically modified microorganisms to create and maintain an energy cycle as seen on our world of origin. Over time, the ground sprouts green and the internal system becomes balanced and self-sustaining.

At least, that is the theory. As of this writing, no planet has become completely self-reliant. Part of it is the prerequisite to continually import new microorganisms and soil directly from Earth to bolster what already exists at the colonies. The other side is the necessity to physically work at maintaining an atmosphere and viable planetside so that it does not just dissipate. On the typical successful colony, more than half the population is employed in one way or another at just keeping the place alive. Even the slightest imbalance can cause runaway processes that end up killing everyone and return the planet to its prior state.

This is known as "colony collapse", and it has happened many times in the past. It is most likely to occur in the initial year, which is why Quantum Ship missions to new colonies typically have a layover of at least that long (along with the need to build their own refueling station and then use it). After that year, the probability decreases significantly, but has never reached anywhere near zero. When I asked Marco Chung about this, he told me that it was "like the planet [was] rejecting having life on it, as if it doesn't belong."

Yet even after colony collapse, that is not necessarily the end. An assessment will determine if the world should be attempted again. If a colony failed in year one, a post-mission analysis will usually find that there was a factor that was missed that made the world unsuitable in the first place, and that data will be synthesized in order to update the criteria used to filter through potential exoplanets in the future. On the other hand, if a planet was successful for ten or more years and then fell apart due to human error, those types of worlds are just too rare to leave vacant and idle. A recolonization mission will be organized to build over the ashes of its former occupants' ruins.

RECORD #18: PANIC
EMERGENCY BROADCAST, ALL BANDS

"Oh, ho, ho, ho, ho, that is too funny, Jaimé," Veronica Dubois was chuckling in response to her co-host Jaimé Ayuda. "Well, coming up ne—" Veronica suddenly stopped speaking mid-sentence, abandoning what she had planned as her face contorted into a scowl.

"What is it?" Jaimé asked.

"Shhhhh," Veronica commanded as she kept her hand to her ear. "Everyone, we are switching over to an emergency broadcast from Earth Central Command. This is completely unbeli—"

Whatever Veronica was going to say has been lost forever as the feed suddenly shifted to a black screen with a single line of text scrolling across it. The words traversing the nothingness simply stated, "This is an emergency message from Earth Central Command. This is not a test. Please stand by." The message repeated in a loop several times before it cut over to a stark man sitting by himself behind a messy desk. The first words he uttered were, "Am I live?"

Someone out-of-view apparently affirmed the answer to that question as the still unidentified man cleared his throat and began speaking. "Hello, I am David Clarke, Director of the Human Space Agency. Approximately three days ago, we lost communication and access control to all Quantum Ships in orbit around Earth. At first, we thought this was merely a computer glitch associated with the ongoing upgrades, but our unsuccessful efforts to reestablish command have made it clear that this was intentional malfeasance. Can we cut to observational satellite H2217b?"

At that request, the scene shifted to a partial shot of the Earth. In the frame were a handful of Quantum Ships, seemingly doing nothing.

"What you are seeing here," David's voice narrated over the picture, "are several Quantum Ships that are not under our authority anymore. More so, if you look closely, you can see that they are firing their maneuvering thrusters. These actions are not what would be expected from a random malfunction; someone is operating the entire fleet simultaneously using a method we have not yet been able to determine."

As the view cut back to David he continued, "The ships are not just orbiting around Earth anymore, either. Although their onboard tracking programs and hardware seem to have been disabled, our observational satellites have located the spacecrafts all over the solar system. We have seen some around Luna, Mars, Venus, and other solar colonies like those in the Asteroid Belt and on the moons of Jupiter. Due to the limitations of how long it takes light and information to travel, we do not know the exact locations of all of the ships in real-time, but we have spotted them heading further abroad towards the outer reaches of the solar system. Based on what we have garnered locally, we can only assume they are going to or are already in the process of taking up similar positions on more distant bodies.

"What we can ascertain is that no human can possibly be aboard. In order to reach their apparent destinations so quickly, the ships have been running their Torch Drives at incredible speeds, the equivalent of 50Gs. No living being could survive something like that for more than a few moments, so we are confident that they are running on some type of autonomous program, perhaps a hack or virus or a sophisticated A.I. of some kind, or some combination of the three. More importantly, that means that we will also be able to overcome their malignant programming with remote commands as soon as we can establish an uplink.

"A significant minority of the ships are currently parked in orbit near Mercury for reasons that are unclear... not that where any of them are makes that much sense, either. However, given their apparent destinations, we have reason to believe this is nothing but simple theft; that some faction or group of factions is trying to take control of the Quantum Fleet for their own selfish purposes. Earth Central Command has shared intelligence with us in the past about such organizations that do not believe in the safety protocols imposed by the Terran government. They may even be related to political assemblies from the extrasolar colonies that want a Quantum Fleet of their own.

"At this time, we have high confidence in the current or intended position of all Quantum Ships except for one. That single vessel was spotted exiting the Sol System at a nominal velocity, leaving us to believe it must have at least one human occupant. To our great sorrow, we have a pretty good idea of who that could be: none other than HSA's own Marco Chung.

"Captain Chung was recently approved to join an upcoming mission and was provided a special dispensation to visit his expected assigned ship in order to oversee the finishing touches on the repairs and upgrades. This extraordinary permission was granted despite him not having fully completed his mandatory entire year on Earth. Given his advanced age and declining physical condition, it was determined that the risk to his overall biology was negligible. That said, and to my eternal shame, I must accept complete responsibility for not considering Captain Chung's mental state and failing to have him partake in a thorough and complete psychological evaluation ahead of time.

"From interviewing workers who were aboard the craft that was commandeered, we learned that Captain Chung declared some type of safety issue and ordered everyone off of the ship and onto the docking platform. This command was also carried over to all other Quantum Ships so that no other people remained on any vessel. Marco Chung was alone on a single craft and all others had been abandoned by his orders. Additionally, being able to fly a Quantum Ship solo—and, more so, manage multiple ships remotely—requires an extremely specialized skillset, competencies that few in existence even possess. If there was some type of third party that was trying to coerce Captain Chung, Marco knows emergency procedures and coded communication techniques well enough that he would have been able to easily disable the ship before anything untoward happened and send a signal and status to HSA. Therefore, given his lack of execution on any of this, we must assume that he is complicit in all that is transpiring, perhaps even a ringleader.

"HSA has received no messages or demands, so we cannot make suppositions as to his final intent. While this is all very distressing, I must stress that there is no imminent danger. We are asking everyone at this time not to panic and to continue to go about your normal daily activities. After exhaustive consultations with Earth

Central Command and the Terran government, we all decided it would be prudent to be transparent with the community about what is happening. Amateur astronomers have already spotted signs that something was amiss, and we wanted to make sure the complete truth was out there before conspiracy theories took over.

"I emphasize that you should only trust information about this matter that comes directly from HSA, Earth Central Command, or the Terran government. Those spreading misinformation and sowing discord are acting inappropriately and are the only true threat at this time. We are already doing everything within our power, and you can count on us to always have the best interests of the people of Earth and the Sol System in mind with every decision we have made and will make going forward."

Director Clarke paused for a short moment as his eyes darted left and right, possibly reading something on a teleprompter in front of him. He took a breath and concluded, "At this time, I would now like to turn things over to President Rinat for further remarks and instructions."

At that, David Clarke stopped talking and folded his hands on the desk in front of him. He silently stared at the camera for several more Earth-seconds before the scene finally shifted to a dark-haired woman also sitting behind a desk, albeit one far more ornate. Behind her was a flag bearing an emblem of the Earth itself on it. She, too, was quiet for a number of seconds before she started speaking.

"My fellow Earthers, and humans all over the Sol System," President Rinat began, "what Director Clarke has just shared with you is disturbing and frightening, but I want to assure you that I and rest of the Terran government do have this situation well in hand. I want to reiterate Director Clarke's message that there is no need for great concern at this time. We have many more avenues to pursue before anything potentially perilous happens. As I speak, Earth Central Command is taking direct control over all HSA facilities and capabilities. Everyone in the public and private sector will be working together to bring this to a safe and peaceful resolution.

"Now I want to be clear about our intentions in order to assuage any lingering doubts and worries you may have. Earth Central Command will not—I repeat, will not—be firing upon the Quantum Fleet. No one in my government would want to take any action that would endanger any Quantum Ship because doing so will also put all of the people in the colonies in a precarious situation. The Human Expansion Program is completely dependent upon these ships and taking even one out of commission could put an entire world at risk. That is simply too high of a cost and is an action we would only take as a last resort after all other options have failed.

"And I must repeat that there is no active threat at this time. None of the ships have moved into any type of position that could be considered aggressive; and even if they did, they lack any type of offensive weaponry. It would actually be more hazardous to fire upon them as it may set off a chain reaction that could activate a Quantum Shift. As you are well aware, doing so within a solar system could be extremely hazardous. Nevertheless, we have prepared contingency plans even for this potentiality.

"As your President, I am asking for calm, patience, and order while we explore all potential solutions. This includes attempting to contact the missing ship that Marco Chung is allegedly piloting. Every second that goes by, that ship gets further away and the longer it takes for messages to reach him and be returned. As such, even this activity cannot happen instantaneously. Alas, these are the laws of the universe that we must follow and cannot overcome.

"However, we are taking other immediate actions. By my executive authority as President, I am declaring a state of emergency and issuing the following orders. All space elevators are to be immediately locked down—no one is to go up and no one is to come down. Further, no Torch Ship is to leave its current dock and any Torch Ship currently en route is to detour to the nearest port and stay there. I am well aware of the difficulties in suddenly changing velocity and direction when in a locked-in course, but it is a necessary inconvenience to regain control over our system.

"By a similar reasoning, I am taking the unfortunate step of temporarily suspending all private satellite communication and surveillance systems for an indefinite period of time. Only

Earth Central Command Torch Ships, satellites, and other assets will be allowed to function in outer space in order to maintain the utmost efficiency in this time of crisis.

"Thank you for your attention to this matter, citizens, and please stand by for further details and, potentially, additional orders I may make under emergency authorization. In the meantime, the greatest danger, as always, emanates directly from individuals who do not follow directions and spread fake news. We are counting on all of you to do the right thing, and report anyone who is not to the authorities. Soon, we will get through this and everything will return to normal, expected, and predictable ways. You can count on me and my administration to resolve this unprecedented situation quickly and effectively."

RECORD #19: ADIEU

There was no sound as the entirety of the lighted side of the Earth lay in the middle of the frame. The metadata embedded in the video feed indicated it was coming from the "Earth-Sol Lagrange Point 1 Climate Observatory (ESLP1CO)". A later chapter in the book <u>Life x Universe</u> had explained that there were several spots in space where the gravitational pull between two bodies cancelled out, thus making some relatively stable locations where another object could be placed without having to worry about it moving around too much. The Earth-Sol Lagrange Point 1 was one such site sitting about 1.5 million kilometers away from the Earth towards its sun—although some people considered it rather unstable since ESLP1CO occasionally needed to manually adjust its position to stay put.

ESLP1CO ran a continuous video feed of the entire sun-facing side of the Earth while also keeping Sol in view on its backside. Through an advanced artificial intelligence, it provided important data, feedback, and instructions back to the people on Earth to prepare them for weather threats—no matter if those came from terrestrial or solar sources. Afterall, although mankind had been able to take control over much of the galaxy, stars still occasionally just erupted with solar flares of their own volition; rather unpredictably, too. Some things were just beyond human capabilities, at least at that point in their development. Still, they took what precautions they could and tried to stay vigilant using tools like ESLP1CO.

In the silence of space, ESLP1CO's A.I. watched intently as some large, bright blobs moved into equidistant positions in geosynchronous orbit around Earth. Some had traveled to the far side of the planet and were no longer visible, but it could be envisaged that they were in similar positions on the opposite part of the globe. The blobs themselves were not bright; that was just the reflection of the sun off of their shiny metal exteriors. But the resolution on ESLP1CO's cameras was not good enough to make out what those blobs could be. They were simply too far away. Besides, ESLP1CO's job was not to keep track of random bits of things in space, but to watch the Earth in its entirety and report back any concerns. Thus, there was nothing here that was within ESLP1CO's purview or responsibility.

Then, suddenly, ESLP1CO registered an energy spike. Normally, something of this magnitude would be coming from the Sol-side, so having it originate from the Earth-side caused some confusion in its programming. After compensating for the input, ESLP1CO tried to transmit a warning, but there were no scenarios to explain what to do in this situation. Even if ESLP1CO sent a message to Earth Central Command, the energy source was closer and would do its potential damage before the message arrived. Resigned, ESLP1CO opted to just continue recording so that the raw data could be analyzed by its human handlers at a later time.

Someone on Earth must have realized that something was amiss. Several of the large blobs suddenly splintered into many smaller blobs, some so small that ESLP1CO could no longer see them in the human-visible spectrum. In infrared, they continued to burn brightly, although they were difficult to discern from each other.

Despite several of the blobs appearing to be destroyed, many more remained. They all started to become out of focus and ESLP1CO could find no way to compensate. Registering the error, ESLP1CO continued to watch from the quiet of deep space. Unfortunately, the error then grew and the fuzziness seemed to engulf the entire planet.

And then, suddenly, the Earth was not there.

It had been right there a moment before, even down to the smallest nanosecond timeframe that ESLP1CO was recording. ESLP1CO checked its logs and position, attempting to reset its heading and make sure it was pointed at the Earth. Just as it was doing that, it detected a very low-level gravitation wave, almost too small to be noticed. But it was unlike any wave ESLP1CO or any of its similar brethren had ever seen. All the frequencies and harmonics were in reverse, like the wave was pulling instead of pushing. ESLP1CO did not have the proper instruments to handle the input and forwarded the details on to another satellite that was more specialized in this type of thing.

Then, just as suddenly, ESLP1CO found itself spinning out of control. Tumbling head over heels, it could not manage to stabilize itself or get its bearings. ESLP1CO reasoned that it must no longer be at Lagrange Point 1—that it somehow had fallen or been pushed out of its designated location—because it now found itself in an unstable revolution. Even though it continued to try to record, it could not focus its instruments on anything as the input was changing too rapidly. But it had determined that it was on a new trajectory that would eventually crash it into Sol. Not right away, but in the grand scheme of the universe, what was a few thousand years?

Over the next several hours and days, ESLP1CO registered several more of the small-scale reverse gravitational waves. It also briefly captured in its video feed a massive coronal ejection from the sun. It tried to send a warning to the Earth and even the other colonies like Venus, Mars, Luna, the spinning asteroids, and the outer moons, but its antennae were facing the wrong direction and it could not get a lock on any of them. ESLP1CO was alone and on a slow, tumbling death spiral. All it could hope for was some type of miracle rescue. Surely those back on Earth knew its plight and would come to its aid before it was too late.

ANNIHILATION

Record #20: Visitor

For your immediate attention:

Citizens of Proxima Centauri B, as you are aware, last week our long-range sensors detected the unmistakable signature of a Quantum Drive. It appeared at a spot that would be expected for a mission from Earth. However, as reported at that time, the next scheduled ship is still several years away and we have received no messages from Earth indicating otherwise. Abrupt changes to the program have happened in the past, but they generally remain quite rare.

Over the past week, we have been able to track the object and can confirm that it is acting and running at velocities consistent with how a Quantum Ship would operate; namely, that it was traveling at 0.87c and is slowing down. Obviously, due to the speed of light, what we are seeing is where the object was a year ago. As such, it would take 1.7 years for the object to arrive and enter orbital insertion in our system—

meaning that we can expect to have a visitor at Proxima Centauri in approximately eight and a half months from now.

The government is well aware of the consternation the sudden appearance of this object has caused. We have heard all the same rumors that this could be anything, up to and including alien life. Despite our pleas to refrain from speculation and to remain calm until more information could be gleaned, some rabblerousers chose to continue to spread unsubstantiated fear and false information. This has caused material damage to our colony, which—we will explain again—needs to be maintained in a carefully crafted balance to account for our common survival. Anarchial actions are the real danger to our lives, which is why we were forced to put the entire colony in lockdown level three. While we in the government did not enjoy having to take these steps, it was necessary for public safety. Those who have been detained will be charged under the highest statutes the law allows and will face the harshest penalties for their transgressions.

This is especially pertinent because this morning we received a message from the object itself, clarifying what is happening. Attached to this bulletin is a video message from Captain Marco Chung of the HSA Quantum Fleet. For those who are unaware, Captain Chung is also known as the "oldest human in the universe" due to his years of time dilation and service, which even precede the advent of the Quantum Drive. As a matter of fact, Captain Chung first visited us here at Proxima Centauri B around 300 years ago during his first tour of duty. He has a long, rich history with our colony and our people.

In the dispatch, Captain Chung let us know that in recognition for his centuries of service he was "given" a Quantum Ship of his own. Or, as Captain Chung himself said, "Well, given is a bit of stretch. We agreed that I would forgo all of my earnings in exchange for this little gift [that being, a ship of his own]." Captain Chung then went on to explain that this was one of the older vessels that was going to be decommissioned anyway, so it was no big loss to the Human Space Agency. As part of their agreement, Captain Chung will be spending the rest of his days on a "goodwill tour" of sorts, visiting all of the colonies he had a hand in either creating or helping to develop, starting with us right here at Proxima Centauri B—a great honor!

Due to his advanced age, Captain Chung has indicated that he does not intend to stay the traditional full year that is commensurate with any mission. Instead, he will come down our space elevator only long enough to finalize repairs, refuel the ship, and take on supplies. As an independent agent, Captain Chung intends to pay and barter for material goods directly, therefore those businesses that deal with such wares should prepare for a special customer.

Further, Captain Chung has said that he is also willing to take on merchandise that would be desired by another colony. This is a rare opportunity for us and the other colonies to make a direct trade as everything has always had to go through Earth in a hub-and-spoke system. If successful, this could go a long way towards the Terran government and HSA allowing us to have Quantum Ships that go between colonies without an intermediary. Demonstrating that this can be successful is critical for our long-term future, therefore we are encouraging all merchants and artisans to provide their commodities at or below cost. We in the Proxima Centauri Managing Council are preparing legislation that will properly compensate you for any short-term losses and ensure you are made whole.

We encourage you to watch the entirety of Captain Marco Chung's video message and also familiarize yourself with his history in our local Archives. Several links, articles, and other media have been attached below for your edification. Knowledge of his interests will be beneficial in the negotiations effort and help ensure a desirable outcome for us and our aspirations.

In the meantime, we will plan to roll out the red carpet for Captain Chung and will pull out all the stops in order to make sure he is appropriately welcomed here.

RECORD #21: SURVIVAL

Marco Chung stared directly into the camera lens for a moment before saying, "Ship's Log. Date..." and then trailed off.

Marco's nearly unblinking eyes kept their piercing gaze focused directly ahead for several more seconds, saying nothing more. He looked away, then turned back towards the unseen viewers, apparently recomposed. Continuing, he said, "I guess a calendar based on Earth's rotation around the sun no longer applies."

The log entry ended after that and the next one would not come until several days later. Marco began similarly, but then commenced talking some more. "I'm not sure who I am making these logs for? Assuming I am successful, no life will remain. I guess some habits just don't want to die. There's no one to talk to here except the A.I. programs, and I've spoken with them enough over the years that I have a pretty good idea what they are going to say before they open their digitalized mouths.

"There is a lot for me to do in order to maintain the ship without a crew, but it is not like it is all encompassing. Automated systems do most of the hard work and, being only one person, I certainly don't create a lot of strain on the internal environment. This all means that I still have plenty of downtime to use as I see fit. Nevertheless, I can only do so much planning for the duration of my entire mission. Overpreparing might actually be detrimental; I'll need to remain nimble and be able to improvise. People are rather difficult to predict, so I'll have to stay on my toes and not get complacent.

"More so, I'll have to continue to work on my social niceties just like Captain Hersch taught me to do when I was much younger. Although, now it is much more important to do so in order to stay above any suspicion. I've never really been that good with other humans, so it is taking a lot out of me just to keep up with my exercises. Practice is necessary so that my skills do not atrophy from lack of use. Perhaps I should have brought some Sixth Dayers with me to have someone to continue to do training sessions with?"

After a long pause seemingly doing nothing, Marco suddenly said, "No, on second thought, that would have been a bad idea. They would not have understood. It would have ended poorly."

That edition of the log ended there with no warning. After this, the check-ins became more mechanical and technical, what would normally be reported on the ship's overall status. Most interesting among these came about 1.3 ship-years into the journey. That one in particular was about the difficulty of flipping the Torch Drive without any crew to help. Marco had apparently prepared as well as possible to ensure that no gears would get stuck and had robotic helpers nearby at critical crux points in case they did. The turnover actually went smoothly without incident, a testament to his skillset and readiness.

After that, the last log of any importance came just a day later. Again, Marco was alone at his chair on the bridge of the Quantum Ship with the camera facing him. This time, he explained that he had just sent his message to Proxima Centauri B, so the die was now cast.

"I had no choice but to go to Plan B first," Marco complained. "Because of its distance from

Earth, it would receive a message before any of the other colonies. And let's make no mistake about it—Earth Central Command, the Terran government, HSA, and plenty of others undoubtedly sent out messages and data of some kind before they were destroyed. There are repeaters everywhere in the direction of the colonies and eventually these pleas will reach someone. The data is heading out in a bubble-shaped trajectory from Earth at a sub-light speed, so I must stay ahead of it. As such, I have a fairly strict timetable for eliminating the closer colonies, with a small contingency built in. There is an optimal route for this and I have run thousands of simulations in order to make sure I stay on it, including if and when things go wrong.

"This is especially true with the colonies that are fairly close to each other. All of them are capable of transmitting a deep space signal, so I must also take into account the chance they'll be able to send a communication to their relatively nearby neighbors. With all those overlapping bubbles projecting outward, it is going to be very close for a while. Somehow, when this is over, I'll have to find a way to go back and take out as many of those repeaters as possible. However, in every scenario I have run, I have never been able to get them all. I guess it will have to be what it is and I'll let the universe take care of them on its own timetable. After all, killing the remnants of humanity and all Earth-based life is my mission's primary objective.

"Eventually, though, I'll get so far beyond the bubbles that it will no longer matter. Then I'll have to start dealing with the other problem: the fact that other Quantum Ships are not showing up when they are supposed to. The expected schedule for the next tour was delivered in the last runs, so everyone knows around when they are going to have their visits. I can certainly pretend to be those vessels for a while, but pretty soon it will get to the point where I am years behind when someone else should have come. It is going to get hairy.

"Sadly, subterfuge is necessary because I will need fuel and supplies in order to survive and continue onwards. As much as it disgusts me, I must remain alive long enough to see this through to completion. News on Earth's destruction should reach Plan B approximately ten to eleven months after I arrive there, so I absolutely must get everything done well before that point. None of the others will be this razor-thin of a margin, but I'll never be able to rest on my laurels."

Record #22: Trend

It's the latest craze to hit Plan B: Writing!

Upon arriving from Earth in his private retirement Quantum Ship, Captain Marco Chung brought with him a large volume of very rare commodities for trade. Among all of those items, nothing has been as popular as bound paper, pens, and pencils. As such, Captain Chung has been exchanging them prodigiously in his hunt for appropriate goods that he either plans to personally use or barter with on the other colonies in the future.

Since the founding of the Proxima Centauri B colony centuries ago, it has not been the culture of our people to collect "things" or create waste. Particularly, all writing has been done digitally either through typing, voice-to-text, or handwriting using e-ink devices. Even drawing has been relegated to the digital realm! This same thought process was exported to all other extrasolar settlements as it assures the safekeeping of all creations and records and makes them easily backed up and transmissible to the entire galaxy.

But because their lives have always been so completely computerized, the younger generation has expressed a desire for the physical items that they generally lack. Said an adolescent who was seen making sketches in one of Captain Chung's wares, "Everything in life is so ethereal. I just wanted something that was real and was only mine!"

Attitudes like this have caused some consternation among the members of the Proxima Centauri Managing Council. In a general statement to the populous that did not directly address the issue, the Council said that "in a collectivist society like ours, it is important to remember that too much individuality and separation from the pack can lead to very real consequences, up to and including total colony collapse and the death of all we hold dear." Later, when discussing the trend during a broadcasted Council meeting, several members expressed concern that people may forget or refuse to recycle their pens when they run dry or their pencils when they break. All of these items contain highly desirable hydrocarbons, so breaking them down into their molecular components for use elsewhere would be the preferred route.

Others have pointed to more basic logistical issues. If people are recording their thoughts "offline", they contend, then the colony's chronicles will not be in sync and the central database will have a "blind spot". Algorithmic projection is one of the key tools all colonies use to stay safe, and having good data on the actions and thoughts of people is an important part of that.

There is also another worry that Marco Chung has actually flooded the market and created a glut, which could lead to vast amounts of waste and refuse that the colony cannot absorb. A resident historian compared this to Mansa Musa's infamous pilgrimage between Earth locales Mali and Mecca in 1324 CE. Along the way, the extraordinarily wealthy ruler spent and handed out so much gold at every stop that he actually depreciated the value of the precious metal for much of the world.

RECORD #23: GANTT

EXCERPT FROM A HANDWRITTEN DIARY

The Sixth Dayers used to tell me all the time that "God created the Earth and the Heavens, but the Heavens are not for man. We must be humble and make do with the soil God has given us." I do agree that man is not made for the stars, but neither is he meant for Earth. Life is a scourge on the universe in general.

Still, I can't help but reflect on the fact that if people listened to the Sixth Dayers, then I would not have been able to do what was necessary. Maybe I would never have even arrived at my revelation. Most likely I would have died in Puerta Estrella during some back-alley deal gone wrong. Or would Puerta Estrella even exist? When I first got involved with interstellar travel, there were barely a handful of Sixth Dayers out there. Actually, they weren't even "The Holy Church of the Sixth Day Reclamation" back then; just a bunch of loosely connected religious conspiracy nutjobs sharing thoughts with each other online. They didn't have an official name or anything like that. It took them centuries to formalize their teachings and get as large, organized, and well-funded as they became. If that had happened sooner, especially before the Quantum Shift breakthrough, then perhaps things would have ended up differently.

But playing games of "what if" was something that fantasy authors liked to do, oftentimes with the idea that there are multiple universes out there where anything that can happen, does happen. If there really is a multiverse, it is not filled with parallel realities based on our own cosmos that only differ by a mere choice. What hubris to think that if some single human went left or right that it would spawn an entirely new existence! Electrons decide infinite times a nanosecond whether to spin left or right. Did anyone talk about whether those were spurring more universes? Of course not! Humans believed themselves to be so important that their very existence could bring about creation itself!

They did not see that in a multiverse all that matters is the individual universe as its own being. Mankind was an invader, an infection that was already causing a rot from the inside. Humans and all of life were a mistake that needed to be eradicated. Otherwise, how else could the universe stay healthy and compete with all the other universes out there?

The universe does not need nor want life to exist. Contrarily, life was actually getting in the way of the natural order and lifecycles of the universe itself. Whatever error in chemistry led to life emerging on Earth was unique to that planet, that much is obvious now. Perhaps if humans had stayed put like the Sixth Dayers wanted, the disease could have been contained for its limited existence. Yet, by spreading that cancer and violently forcing other virgin bodies to bend to their desires against the will of the universe, it became clear that humanity had to be stopped.

No, the Sixth Dayers would certainly not understand, and would not have agreed with my approach—at least, not those sitting on the High Priest Council. They were, generally speaking, not violent people; quite the opposite, actually. If they had any inkling of what I had them doing, they would have rejected me and turned me over to the authorities. Despite what some people assumed, they weren't idiots. Even their scripture was quite clear that irrespective of their name, they thought of the Genesis story as a parable of what really occurred over billions of years, albeit one directed by the hand of God. It took a lot of effort to string them along, but I indisputably needed their help.

Using my immense resources from my centuries of working for HSA, I was able to hire programmers, gray-hat hackers, machinists, manufacturers, and more to help develop the modules that would give me complete control over the entire Quantum Fleet—especially with the remote process and predetermined sequencing that were critical in pulling this all off. All the work was entirely done by disconnected cells over decades. None of them knew what they were working on in totality; none of them knew what they were giving me; none of them even knew it was me who was paying for it all!

But how to get the modules installed? For that, I needed the Sixth Dayers. More so, I needed able bodied people who would not ask questions and could install the units without anyone noticing. This massive retrofit and upgrade HSA announced provided the one-and-only opportunity when I would be able to undertake this endeavor. With the scheduled maintenance and plan to work on all of the ships at once while, at the same time, finishing up building the new ones, HSA was extraordinarily shorthanded. Employment requirements and background checks were loosened in order to get enough warm bodies up the elevator. True, I had to use some of my hacker acquaintances to clean up the records for a few Sixth Dayers, but that was simple enough considering the lack of detailed checks HSA was doing during their hiring frenzy.

Hilariously, I even heard Jaimé Ayuda—of all people—plugging the job openings during a replay of that so-called "Interstellar Parade". That dick, he was a real pain in my ass. He got way too close to the truth. If anyone ever took him seriously, I might have even been in real trouble. Well, I suppose I can thank Veronica for keeping him out my hair...

Anyway, the grunts on the ground (in space?) did what they were ordered based on blind faith. People like the Chief Missionary had to be told something, so I sold him a bill of goods about how the modules would permanently disable the Quantum Ships without harming anyone. He wanted me to "officially" come out as a Sixth Dayer so badly that he was willing to overlook just about anything. I think his job was on the line, too, and he was scrambling to save his own position. He saw what transpired with his former boss and knew the same could happen to him if he failed to deliver something huge. And who would have been a bigger catch than me?

With the modules installed and me finally allowed to ascend the space elevator, I was able to put my plan in motion. For "Phase 1", it was absolutely necessary to make sure the inner Sol System was taken out as quickly as possible because they were the only ones that could potentially mount a planetary-level defense. I had to use a great number of the ships around Earth, Luna, Mars, and Venus to ensure that those places were fully accounted for. With that much redundancy, it was not a major issue to Quantum Shift each of those worlds into their sun. Yes, the effort destroyed all of those otherwise still useful ships with the planets, but it was worth the sacrifice because that single action terminated 90% of humanity in one fell swoop.

Oh, that's right, no one realized that it was now possible to get a Quantum Field originating on one ship to be the size of an entire planet, at least not with their prior understanding of the technology. That was another one of my innovations. HSA had no idea that I actually knew how the Quantum Shift worked, nor that I had figured out how to expand the field. They didn't have a clue about what I was doing during my years and years spent between worlds with nothing but time on my hands. Secretly, I used those boundless stretches to learn from the true experts and put all the pieces together. But that is not my most important contribution to the subject of quantum-based travel.

No, I have achieved a far greater leap, an advancement that finally made this mission possible! I can now program the Quantum Shift so that the ship goes one direction and the target world goes another. Thus, while I may have needed almost the entire Quantum Fleet to take out the Sol System, this one vessel will be more than adequate for obliterating the remainder of the colonies.

On the "Planet Blah" social media platform, the denizens of Proxima Centauri B took to message boards to generally complain about their dull existences. While it certainly seemed cathartic for them to grumble about their lot in life, there did not appear to be any indication that it led to any tangible results. Due to living under the surface of the planet in a precariously balanced system, any feats of real defiance were considered tantamount to attempted mass murder and were punished just as harshly for the alleged offense by the iron fist of the Proxima Centauri Managing Council.

Still, the Council appeared to tolerate the existence of this application, and in many ways, one could say, encouraged its use. Based upon recorded sessions of Council meetings, it was clear that there was initially disagreement on whether Planet Blah should be allowed to continue. However, on the whole, it was decided that it was better for the people to vent online with harmless words than to engage in any concrete acts of rebelliousness. As Planet Blah continued its existence and expanded its user base, the Council was happy to note that the content basically became frivolous and inconsequential, just the type of thing they were hoping for in order to create a distraction away from the real issues affecting the colony.

One such thread was entitled "Why won't Marco Chung take me with him?" It began with a single person complaining about how they approached Captain Chung with the idea of joining Marco aboard the Quantum Ship and, once there, to serve as a deckhand. After all, the individual remarked, it must be quite difficult to maintain and run the ship all by himself. "Besides," the user wrote, "it's just like the government said in the bulletin: we should offer everything we can and help try to make intra-colony journeys and trade a reality!"

As others began to chime in and agree, further stories of encounters with Marco Chung began to pop up. A teenage street urchin explained to Marco that she and her friends wanted nothing more than to get "out of these back-woods" and that they had no prospects or future on Proxima Centauri B. They thought Marco would understand, having come from nothing himself, but he would not be swayed.

This prompted an actual orphan to enter into the conversation. The orphan said that they thought that "Marco would be more sympathetic [to them] given [their] similar origins." Going on for a while, the orphan conceded that they now felt even more abandoned and rejected. Others in the chat told the orphan to reach out to them in private messages, and that they would like to help them. Since the orphan did not post any-where on Planet Blah again, it is impossible to know if they took them up on the offer.

There then came some pushback from among the users, calling the original poster a "beggar" who "was not offering anything to Marco Chung in return." These users claimed the others would just be a burden on a geriatric retiree and that they had to come up with a different approach, one in which they could actually offer Marco Chung something he needed or wanted.

In retort to this, a large number of people

shared their aptitude exam scores, advanced degrees, relevant work experiences, and other similar measures. All reported that they were equally rebuffed. There did not seem to be anything that Marco was willing to accept and they were beginning to sour on his image of being some type of folk hero. "What did he ever do," someone asked, "aside from grow old and drive a space bus?"

All of these mounting failures to sway Marco's stance did not seem to dissuade people from taking alternate approaches. One user posted that she had "dried up the entire dating pool on this planet and was hoping [she] would hit it off with Marco. In any case, isn't he lonely up there? Doesn't he want some company?"

The conversation veered towards rumors of Marco's prolific interest in the female gender. It was well known among the inhabitants of Plan B that when then-Deckhand Chung had first come to their planet nearly 300 years ago, he had left quite a few broken hearts in his wake. Someone joked that maybe he wasn't interested because she was actually his descendant. Later, some killjoy reminded everyone that the entire colony's

DNA profile was publicly available in order to avoid inbreeding. "Duh" was the response to that post that got the most likes.

"How about this," one woman offered. "You have to realize that Marco has been around the block a few times, so we need to propose something he has never had before. What if a bunch of us ladies went up with him and we filmed a no-limits dating show? We could call it 'Love Amongst the Stars' and sell the distribution rights to every colony we visit. Sounds good, doesn't it?"

A poll was put up to determine if "Love Amongst the Stars" was a viable idea, and it won with 63% of the participating vote. However, one woman doubted that Marco would ever take them up on the offer. By her account, she had run into Marco and had "literally thrown [herself] at him, offered him his wildest sexual fantasies, and he just pushed [her] away!"

Some of the young males in the thread began to deride this woman, claiming that she was probably just ugly. They then began to pester her, demanding a naked picture. For indeterminate reasons, she acquiesced to this harassment and provided a nude photo of herself, albeit with her head removed. This led to a lot of catcalls and what could loosely be termed "compliments". "I'd do you!" one teenage boy offered. Another posted a picture of his erect penis with the caption "You can ride on my rocket!"

With the thread obviously spiraling out of control and away from the original topic, engagement started to drop off. After a while, it would be days before anyone added anything new. The last post on there simply stated, "Maybe he just doesn't like people?"

"And now," the anchor at the news desk said, segueing out of the prior segment, "let's go to Grishma D'Cruze, who is on location at the base of the space elevator. Grishma?"

The scene cut to a woman standing with a microphone in hand in front of some metal girders that must have been part of the support structure for the space elevator. Most likely it was just an extension from the mountain on the surface that the actual line was attached to since it would be unnecessary and certainly not beneficial to bring the actual line underground—especially considering the gravity situation on Proxima Centauri B compared to Earth and the other Earth-analogue colonies.

Behind and around Grishma, a few people were milling about aimlessly. Although it looked like there was a lot of debris on the ground, no one appeared to be cleaning it up. Otherwise, all seemed to be quiet and Grishma could be easily heard from her remote position.

Succeeding a brief pause due to some technical limitation that seemed to cause a delay in communications between her and the studio, Grishma began, "Thanks, Kyung-Hee. Yes, I am here at the access portal to the space elevator where hours ago Marco Chung entered and ascended alone to his waiting Quantum Ship in orbit. Following the completion of refueling and repair efforts at a record pace in less than eight months, Captain Chung had decided to leave and continue his goodwill tour of the colonies. To send him off in style, the Proxima Centauri Managing Council organized a parade in his honor."

The video then cut over to the festivities from earlier with Grishma providing a voiceover and interviewing people in the crowd. The hallway leading away from the main living and commercial districts of the core prefecture on Proxima Centauri B saw thousands of people lined up on each side. As Marco was driven on some type of electric cart with rubberized wheels, people were throwing flower leis, beaded necklaces, and confetti at him.

Marco's mobile contraption putted along at a

slow pace, giving the crowd ample time to throw colorful decorations atop him, which later became the thick layer of litter coating the ground behind Grishma. He was waving to the cheering crowd, but the grimace adorning his face was telling another story entirely. According to Grishma, though, what we were seeing was Marco's best smile, though his advanced age was holding it back from being the amplest possible. Also, she made a supposition that Marco was concerned about the journey ahead and was holding back his sadness at having to leave such a lovely colony.

After the prerecorded segment concerning the parade, the scene cut back to Grishma at her live shoot who said, "By this point, Captain Chung has reached the top of the space elevator and is now aboard his Quantum Ship. Back to you in the studio, Kyung-Hee."

"Thanks for that wonderful report, Grishma," Kyung-Hee declared. "Now, we go live to a camera outside the space elevator docking platform as Marco Chung is about to break orbit and start on the next part of his odyssey."

Kyung-Hee sat smiling at the desk, but

nothing changed. After what felt like an eternity but was most likely just a handful of seconds, Kyung-Hee said, "We appear to be having some technical difficulties with our feed. We'll get you up there as soon as we can. In the meantime..." Kyung-Hee trailed off mid-sentence and put her finger to her ear. Her eyes grew wide as she started yelling, "Wait, what was that? What is happening? No, that can't be ri—"

The broadcast suddenly ended.

Record #26: Scope
Excerpt from a Handwritten Diary

While I have made great strides in Quantum Shift technology, I have to admit that I did not invent anything. I was just clever enough to be able to build upon the work of others before me, ones much smarter and with greater skillsets than I have. If I had not figured out how to do it first, someone else would have come to the same conclusions. And that was another reason I had to act when I did.

Extending the Quantum Field to be as big as an Earth-sized body was the next logical leap that was coming down the pike. Theoretical quantum physicists had already put out academic papers about how they could relocate entire planets to better locations. The use cases were endless—moving an Earth-analogue to the habitable zone of a star; taking a colony like Plan B and bringing it to a G-type sun; dropping Venus into Earth's orbit but on the other side of Sol; saving the Earth itself by pushing its orbit outward as Sol grew;

and so much more. Humans were planning to rearrange the natural order of the universe in order to make it better suited for themselves.

Of course, that has always been the human way. Eons ago, humans stopped rapidly evolving and made one decision: instead of changing themselves, they would modify the environment to be how they liked it. Why would they bother to grow and transform when the better solution was to increase their own ease and comfort? They took this attitude to new lands then to whole other worlds. Failure never stopped them; they just built right on top of the corpses and tried again and again until they bent the universe to their will.

The idea of shifting an entire planet started to enter the public zeitgeist during my last return to Earth. I saw a video by some online personality going by the moniker "FasterThanMach69" who attempted to break down the key points for a generalized audience. I mean, he glossed over a lot of the details and got plenty of them wrong, but the viewer engagement levels were enough to make my skin crawl. It was obvious that the younger generation was excited by these ideas and was going to facilitate efforts to help them come to fruition. The next breakthrough would not have required billions of people to be working on it. It just warranted inspiring the right individual who could then make the essential cosmological connection.

Worst of all, I know it would not have ended there. The size and mass of a planet are one thing, but the same attributes of a star are another level entirely. And to be clear, mass is the key factor because it means more fundamental particles to keep track of. Look no further than Sirius B, a white dwarf 8.6 light-years from Sol. Sirius B is actually smaller in diameter than the Earth was, yet has almost the same mass as Sol. It is just so densely packed in.

That said, wouldn't Sirius B have provided the perfect laboratory setting to find a way to move a Sol-like object? Afterall, once they could shift an Earth-analogue, they'd start to look at bigger and bigger entities. Eventually, they would want to try a star, and there was one nearby that was small in size but just the right mass. Humanity would have literally redrawn the constellations in order to gratify their unsatiable need for dominion, becoming some sort of megalomaniacal "star-builders".

Yes, given enough time, they would have figured it out. I was able to solve the problem for an Earth-massed body, at least for my purposes. Truthfully, I did not have to be very meticulous. Real scientists would have wanted to carefully move a planet; I wanted to destroy them. It actually doesn't matter to me if my methodology is flawed or good or any of those things—it is honestly better for my plan if my way is imperfect and causes substantial damage. All things considered, it is not as if I am trying to perfectly preserve a world before I drop it off into its sun.

Still, even with the leaps I made, I could not do much about Sol itself. The ideal solution would have been to just eliminate or move the humans' sun. All the planets, planetoids, and everything else in the Sol System would have flown off in every direction and died out in short order, unless they collided with each other in the chaos and got taken out early. Either way, there would have been no chance for survival unless they were able to build another Quantum Drive. Given that potentiality, I suppose that removing the inner planets was still the right first move to avoid that conceivable scenario, but it still would have been advantageous to have been able to take that next step by removing the beating heart at the center of their home system.

Instead, what I tried to do was a more piecemeal solution. First, I parked several ships in Mercury's solar orbit—but not around Mercury. Although there were very few people there, I could not chance any of them getting close to one of my modified Quantum Ships as they ran their predetermined programs. When that package executed, though, the ships made several Quantum Shifts around Sol's corona (before plunging themselves directly into the photosphere when their fuel ran low) in an attempt to encourage some type of enormous coronal mass ejection or another type of uncontrollable nuclear chain-reaction.

At least, that is what I assumed happened. I was long gone by that point because I needed to start the journey to Plan B. I still have to treat it like any other "normal" mission and build up the proper velocity, appear in the expected spot, and decelerate. If I just materialize at Proxima

Centauri or anywhere else without any velocity, the jig would be up! No one will believe that HSA has suddenly changed their safety protocols, especially without decades of warning and many beta-test runs in unpopulated environments.

After I shift Plan B into Proxima Centauri, I'll have to do the same procedure again. It will be another excruciatingly slow velocity build to 0.87c, a flip, a deceleration, and an orbital insertion at the next colony. This will be the pattern over and over and over until I am sure they are all gone.

But doing a standing Quantum Shift followed by a "regular" journey that includes its own shift is very taxing on the engines and the fuel supply. Making it to each colony will be much tighter than the standard specs recommend. On top of that, I have to slack on maintenance in order to keep up with the schedule—as well as my own limited remaining years.

Record #27: Garden
Advertisement Video

The camera panned over a babbling brook running through a field of vividly green grass. Trees dotted the landscape in the background as birds could be seen flittering between their branches. Above it all, a blue sky was punctuated with just a couple of small, white fluffy clouds. Sounds emanating from the stream, the avians, and the wind lightly tinkled through the scenery.

A gentle-voiced feminine narrator then said, "What you are seeing here is not some mythical garden of yore. No, everything before you is much, much better—created by the hand of mankind itself into a perfectly engineered paradise. This... is Eden 2!"

At that, a montage of locations around the colony called Eden 2 was presented over a bombastic instrumental track. Most showed wide-open spaces, abundant markets filled with fresh produce, people partaking in outdoor activities like hiking and swimming, animals frolicking, and other tranquil and inviting sights. The camera then changed to a panning drone overview of one of the major cities and followed its unbroken trail as it made a voyage from the metropolis and out to suburbs, exurbs, and then the rural countryside. A woman was waving from below in front of a red barn and the drone turned around and headed towards her.

The image then cut to a closeup shot of the formerly waving woman's face as the musical overture ended and she said, "What do I like best about Eden 2? Well, I guess, I would say just how unlimited the opportunities are!"

The video then started to rapidly shift between other people who also announced their favorite attributes of the colony.

"The clean air!" declared one.

"The freedom!" proclaimed another.

"Open spaces as far as the eye can see!" one person attested.

This went on for a while with many more people asserting all of the wonders of the planet that they could not find on Earth, most of the Sol-based settlements, nor even among some of the recent extrasolar colonies. Finally, one summed it up with, "A chance to start anew!"

The narrator then returned at the conclusion of this segment to present more idyllic views of the planet. "Eden 2 was the first colony on an Earth-analogue around a G-type star, a star just like Earth's sun Sol. Prior to Eden 2, colonization of other worlds was a dreadful experience that led to less than stellar results. At best, people were forced to permanently live underground on bodies that did not have the right gravity, whether it was too little or too much. Either situation literally was physically killing them, but the psychological costs were considerably higher. It is a scientific fact that humans need to see blue skies and green plants, but even on Earth these are hard to come by nowadays."

The pictorials ended as everything shifted into archival footage showing construction in the Asteroid Belt. The narrator continued, "Some people pretended they could solve these core issues by hollowing out asteroids and spinning them up so that the centrifugal force would push the living beings to the edges at a rate close to the gravity on Earth. While it may have solved many of their bodily issues, it could not resolve their emotional and spiritual ones. Looking up and seeing what was essentially the ground on the other side of the asteroid rather than an open sky made their inner life worse—as limited and closed in as their physical one was."

With that, the view repositioned to shots of the horizon of Eden 2. Its sun was in the process of rising, displaying an array of pink, orange, and purple hues giving way to the blue and banishing the grey of the dawn after the darkness of the night. To wit, the narrator simply declared, "The sky." After a short pause lingering on birds singing in a slight breeze, the narrator returned saying, "Eden 2 was the first place to bring a sky to the lost people of Earth and the prior colonies. Over the centuries, millions have flocked here for all of the opportunities and wonders of a new Earth—most of all, one that has not been fractured and overburdened by a history of destructive behavior. However, it is not just Earthers. Even people who thought they were making a 'Plan B' realized that Eden 2 was the bliss that they were seeking, and that this planet is overflowing with the unbridled joy they had been foregoing."

The viewpoint must have been from a steady drone because it suddenly tilted and started flying over fields and forests of green, yellow, red, and other bright colors. Over this, the narrator explained, "Although hundreds of years have passed, there is still plenty of room, prospects, and resources for you, too. You CAN have a home here, no matter where you are starting from, and Eden 2 Relocation Services has generous packages available that will help you make the journey, immigrate, and successfully settle here. Click below for details on what is truly possible when you have the entire surface of a planet to call your own."

A clickable link and scannable code appeared at the bottom of the screen and was also embedded into the metadata and description of the video. The drone video then went towards a mountain in the distance to reveal the line for the space elevator. Flying close to the track and upwards, the drone discovered a trolley coming down filled with people who had their faces pressed to the windows as they waved at the floating camera. After that, the drone headed downward towards the landing area where it could be seen that a trolley that had arrived earlier was disembarking. Standing next to the exiting people was a familiar looking—although quite younger in appearance—man in an HSA uniform. There was another cut to a head-on shot of the HSA employee directing people out of the trolley and officially welcoming them onto the planet's surface.

In this vista, the narrator said, "And here is HSA Quantum Ship Captain Marco Chung welcoming the most recent batch of happy arrivals. Sorry, Captain Chung, it's going to be a long and lonely journey back to Earth since nobody ever wants to leave Eden 2!"

RECORD #28: CURTAIN
PERSONAL RECORDING DEVICE

"Are you recording?" the young man pulling along the person behind the camera asked.

"Yes, yes," a squeaky voice of indeterminate gender responded, "I already told you it's on. Ow! Stop yanking on my arm so hard!"

"Then let's get going, Ezhil," the still unidentified boy demanded. Letting go, he said, "Please, we gotta hurry!"

"I'm already hurrying!" Ezhil complained. "Wanna tell me what this is all about, Torvald?"

"You just gotta see for yourself," Torvald responded. "Okay, there, there, look!"

Ezhil shifted the focus of the camera towards what Torvald was pointing at. Atop of some crates in a back alley sat Marco Chung, surrounded by a group of other local youths assembled cross-legged on the unprotected concrete. With a gasp, Ezhil dropped the recording device and there was a loud clank as it shut off.

"—am so sorry," Ezhil was pleading as the

recording came back online while Torvald continued to scold them. "It's working again!"

"Not me, you idiot," Torvald berated directly into the lens. "Shoot him!"

"Okay, got it!" Ezhil declared as they turned the camera towards Marco. Marco's mouth was moving and he was gesturing about something, but the recorder didn't pick up any sound. "I'm not getting anything..."

"Move closer!" commanded Torvald. "Geez, why do I always have to think for you?"

"Sorry, sorry again!" Ezhil cried.

"Stop being sorry and start getting in there!" Torvald reprimanded.

"I'm going, I'm going!" Ezhil declared before finally starting to move forward towards the semi-circle with Marco at its apex.

"Yeah, this alley reminds me a great deal of where I grew up," Marco was in the middle of saying. "Seeing the rot and decay in this self-described paradise reinforces why what I do is so absolutely necessary."

"What does he mean?" Ezhil whispered.

"Shut up!" Torvald whisper-yelled back.

"What are you two talking about?" Marco

asked Ezhil and Torvald as he turned his attention directly towards them. "Wait, are you recording me?"

"Ummmm, uhhhhh…" was about all that Ezhil could muster. Torvald must have been shellshocked because he said nothing at all.

Making a throat clearing noise, Marco said, "Eh, don't worry about it. You can record whatever you want."

Torvald suddenly found some courage and said, "Well, uh, Mr. Chung, Marco, sir, ummm, would you, uh…"

"Spit it out," Marco insisted, but with a low tone that did not make it sound like the harsh edict it could be.

Torvald spoke at such a rapid pace that all the words sounded like they were one, "Would you please come with us so that we can show you the real and truly horrible underbelly of Eden 2 and record the whole thing so that someone famous like you can raise awareness that there are real problems here and they are completely ignoring them and then you can maybe help bring about change and hope to the hopeless and give us the opportunity for a better future?"

Marco and everyone else in the semi-circle were completely silent. Ezhil almost dropped the camera again seemingly from the tension alone.

"If it's not too much trouble?" Torvald asked, breaking the excruciating silence.

Finally, after another long time with no one saying a word, Marco smirked and said, "Sure, I have the time. What's there to lose?"

Torvald, Ezhil, and the other dissidents took Marco around many other decrepit zones in the out-of-sight areas of Eden 2. They introduced him to unhoused people begging on the street corners until the local constabularies came and picked them up. The police—who were not keen about being on camera—claimed that they were taking them to a shelter so that they could receive help, but Ezhil said that anyone who was taken away was never heard from again.

After that, they broke into the underground maintenance area where all of the power, water, sewage, and other lines and facilities were. Everything was in poor condition and many of the paths they took appeared not to have been visited in a long time, judging by the layers of dust and grime. They came across people who were living in forgotten chambers down there, suffering from common illnesses and conditions that should have been easily treatable given their medical capabilities. There were even children, some with parents, others on their own.

Later, the group visited Torvald and Ezhil's neighborhood, a shanty slum on the outskirts of the city dump. Their homes were little more than one-room shacks, made out of the loose materials that they found amongst the garbage that was being trucked in on a regular basis. "How is it," Torvald asked, "that we could have an entire planet and all the knowledge of human history, and yet still repeat all the same errors and mistakes that were committed on Earth?"

Expecting an answer, Torvald stared at the much older man, clearing his throat when Marco didn't respond at length. "We're not going to have much useful footage if he doesn't ever comment or say why," Ezhil whined.

"Why?!" Marco suddenly screeched in response, rushing towards Ezhil. "Why?! You want to know why?"

"Ye-ye-yes," Ezhil stuttered.

"Because all of this is wrong!" Marco barked

while gesturing his hands in every direction. "Because humans, life, none of it can be trusted. All it can do is destroy and wreak havoc on the universe, and the universe never asked for any of this. This whole world is a lie! If your government stopped maintaining and supporting the atmosphere, the magnetic field, and the rest, you all would be dead in a matter of days. I've seen it happen plenty of times. What? Just because you've been so successful at terraforming you think you're any good? The best of the worst is still complete shit."

At the end of that diatribe, Marco simply walked away, never to be seen by the malcontents again, at least not on the record. "Do you think we can use any of that?" Ezhil asked.

"Don't be stupid," Torvald bit back, "and turn that fucking thing off."

Ezhil did just that.

RECORD #29: CHECK-IN
INTERNAL SHIP LOG

Marco Chung was again staring into the camera lens with the bridge of his Quantum Ship visible behind him. "Ship's Log," be began, "I have just successfully shifted Eden 2 into its sun and begun my journey to Naya Nakshatra under nominal conditions. Per usual, I should arrive in just under 2.6 of my years.

"Of particular importance, I was able to more efficiently complete the turnover process resulting in only a 7.5-month layover at Eden 2. Over the next couple of years, I will be reviewing the data and seeing if there is more time that can be shaved off. Just doing a cursory review of my own notes, I have highlighted several areas that warrant further investigation, some that could result in gains in the days-to-weeks timeframe.

"Unfortunately, economies of scale dictate that each improvement will be subsequently less than the last one. At some point, I am going to run out of possible ways to make this process go any faster. The laws of physics simply prevent me from being able to turn things around in less than four or five months.

"Still, I am hopeful that there is something I can do between worlds that might be able to contract this procedure. If there was some type of fuel generation I could do on board or repairs that could be made while already underway—anything would be beneficial to speeding this whole thing up. I would rather spend as little time as possible planet-side. Being down there fills me with feelings of regret.

"When I was stuck on Eden 2, a group of ne'er-do-wells showed me what was really happening on that planet; not all the glitz and glamour that the government portrayed in their advertisements. All the negligence they had me witness really reinforced just how abusive life is to the natural order of the universe. Worst of all, they wanted to use me as a symbol to further their own cause and bring even more unnatural and disgusting change to their world! As if I would ever be sympathetic to their plight while they were planning to exploit an innocent sphere even more than its erstwhile overlords?!

"I feel so bad for all of the bodies in the galaxy that have been touched by the injurious hands of mankind. They never asked for what happened to them, to have life thrust upon them without their consent. And although the universe itself constantly fought back against these violations, humankind never paid attention and persisted by continuing their caustic path.

"What those people on Eden 2 wanted would have only extended the damage to that precious planet. If I could have just wiped all life from the surface and let that world finally return to its innate state, I would have. I wish I could save these planets that have done no wrong. The death throes of Plan B still haunt me in my sleep, and I know Eden 2 and all the rest will soon join it in my nightmares.

"But like any surgeon, I had a decision to make. Do I try to save the limb and perhaps condemn the body, or do I cut off the limb and ensure the survival of the whole being? I made my choice, and over the vast timespans of the universe it will eventually heal from these small incisions that I have been forced to make."

The log ended there and nothing was

reported again until about 3.2 ship-years later. Marco returned to the recording saying, "Ship's Log: Naya Nakshatra has been successfully shifted into its sun with no notable issues or holdups. At this time, I am underway to Xinjja. Of particular importance, only some of my envisioned efficiency gains in the turnover time were realized, and I am not completely sure why. There are no other experts for me to run scenarios with, so I'll just have to see if I can find improvements in other ways or figure out what went wrong with my intended methods by myself. I'm concerned that maybe there's a gap in my understanding.

"Potentially, there might be some people I could consult with on Xinjja. However, knowing them, they would want to come up to the Quantum Ship and do a detailed inspection and analysis. There is too much risk in allowing anyone aboard, nonetheless, giving them access to critical systems. Also, I cannot look past the possibility that they may want to commandeer the craft for their own purposes. Such attempts have been made in the past among various colonies, all unsuccessfully I might add. HSA learned a lot about the necessity of shipside security after what happened on Venus forever ago.

"No, I may just have to accept that I am pushing the ship beyond its intended usage and lifetime, and that I can't keep up with the maintenance as much as I thought I could. Looking back, maybe I should have tried to get the split-shift solution installed on more ships and given myself a backup inventory of vessels. I could have stationed them at various out-of-the-way spots and moved onto them as the need arose. Ultimately, though, that would have cost more time, and time is my most precious commodity.

"Unfortunately, I believe I am going to have to accept that my layovers are going to get longer, not shorter. The equipment is just going to require more attention as it ages and is subjected to extreme extended use. Of course, I won't give up completely on trying to find ways to get out of dodge as quickly as possible, but I may just be at the mercy of the machinery."

After a similar amount of time, Marco reappeared in the register again. "Ship's log," he said comparably the same as the time before, "Xinjja has been successfully shifted into its sun.

Everything is as nominal as can be considering the difficulty in sustaining the ship. I tried to hire custom fabricators on the planet to build replacement parts, but they lacked the quality level that was available back on Earth and the Sol System in general. Additionally, the necessary experience to work in such exacting specifications based on plans alone just didn't exist there. Although everything they provided is substandard, I have no choice but to use them in order to continue the mission.

"The next stop is Manzil Jadid, which is another reason I chose to attempt some type of manufacturing at Xinjja. Those on Manzil Jadid have pretty much chosen a non-technological based society, aside from what is required to maintain their atmosphere and other considerations. Otherwise, one might say their planet is the least hospitable of all of the colonies. Ironically, though, because of these decisions, Manzil Jadid is as close as a human infested world can be to its natural form. Given that, I feel particularly bad about having to destroy this planet."

Once again there was a gap of years, and once more Marco returned to check in. "Ship's log:

Manzil Jadid has been shifted into its sun. This was one of the easier assignments as the people of this world were relatively uninterested in me. There have been no major developments of note, but I continue to look for ways to improve efficiency and upkeep. While I have been able to stem the bleeding, there does not appear to be any way to reverse the process.

"I am already underway to Atarashi Tochi and do not have any specific concerns or goals for while I am there."

After another break in the recordings for a few years, Marco reentered the scene to say, "Ship's Log: Atarashi Tochi has been successfully shifted into its sun. Nothing significant to report. I am nominally underway to Eretz HaGalut."

Subsequent to that short message, in the following log Marco simply stated, "Eretz HaGalut is complete. I am underway to the next colony. See original plan for detail."

The succeeding log cut things down further as Marco stated with a perfunctory notation, "Mission complete, nominally underway to the next destination."

And so on and so forth they went until the log

itself was apparently no longer worth Marco's time to record even a few measly words. That is, not until much, much later.

EXCERPT FROM THE BOOK <u>LIFE x UNIVERSE</u>

"But what about a moon?" you cry. "Why can't we live on one of those?"

Well, first off, we already do live on moons, at least in the Sol System. One of the earliest colonies in history was on Luna, and in the pre-Quantum Shift times we also built settlements on the satellites of Jupiter and Saturn, including Io which has more mass, size, density, and gravity than Luna. However, that is still a very small sized ball overall, and we quickly learned that places like that lead to low gravity sickness. Humans and all Earth-based life are made for 1G.

Nonetheless, that is just the Sol System, and the Milky Way is vast with possibilities. In some extrasolar systems, we have discovered moons that are Earth-analogues in the mass and gravity department. We often find them in orbit around so-called "Super-Jupiters", a very wide category of planets that ranges anywhere from a little more massive than Jupiter to about 80 Jupiter-masses. Any bigger than that and they tend to collapse into brown dwarfs, what is also known as a "failed star". Brown dwarfs are luminous like main-sequence stars, but they cannot sustain nuclear fusion and therefore cool off pretty quickly, relatively speaking. There is one just 6.5 light-years from Earth, but you'll never see it with regular instruments in the human visual spectrum!

Now, it is important to note that systems like Sol are the outliers. Having small terrestrial objects close to a sun and large icy and gassy ones far out is very abnormal. Most systems have the big planets on the inside, so being able to colonize the moons of these giant worlds would open our options up tremendously.

That said, a lot of Super-Jupiters are of the "hot" variety. These extremely large worlds are exceedingly close to their suns, packed in there so tightly that they would be of no use whatsoever. Imagine trying to survive somewhere even closer to a star than Mercury! We barely maintain a mining operation on Mercury due to the difficult logistics of not being burnt to a crisp, so having a rotating body around another body that is inside an even chummier circle would not be any type of picnic.

So, what about the "cold" variety, where they might even be in the habitable zone of their suns? Sure enough, we have several examples of this exact situation and have explored the possibility of building colonies on them. There is actually quite a lot to like about this setup. For instance, even though previously we talked about having a moon for tidal forces, the Super-Jupiter/Earth-analogue-moon combination essentially replicates that factor quite nicely.

Yet proximity is a considerable problem to contend with. Bigger planets emit more radiation, and most of the time the moons pass right through their radiation belts. Even though they are "cold", these Super-Jupiters can still cook us pretty easily. Although being underground in a place like that would not be great, at least it is potentially doable! Unfortunately, even if the moon is far enough out to avoid the radiation belt that would fry all life, there is usually some other factor that makes it less desirable or probable to sustain a self-functioning colony.

As such, the question simply becomes: why

bother? The whole point of the Human Expansion Program is to be able to live on the surface of a terrestrial body like it is the Earth. This means we want to be on a stand-alone sphere that "feels" like a real planet. We desire nothing less than an idealized version of the home-world we are leaving behind.

RECORD #31: INCOMPLETE
EXCERPT FROM A HANDWRITTEN DIARY

Sometimes I wake up with this feeling of paranoia, like if I look over my shoulder someone will be there. It is not as if I am expecting a stowaway to be aboard the ship; I have thoroughly inspected this vessel and made sure that there were no unexpected stragglers. Even if some crafty human has somehow avoided my omniscient gaze (for am I not the God of this ferry?), I have shut down all life support systems in the areas of the ship that I do not regularly enter. Anyway, doing that fit into my overall energy management plan, though it also had the added benefit of ensuring that no living being save some tardigrades and other extremophiles could possibly survive. Maybe I should consider intentionally creating a radiation leak to clear out those tenacious little buggers, too?

No, the thing I occasionally worry about—unnecessarily, I might add—is a threat from the Sol System. Earth, Luna, Mars, and Venus are definitively gone; I could see that much happen on my way out of the system. And I have every reason to believe that my manipulation of Sol's outer layers roasted Mercury and many other objects in the inner solar system. However, I still sometimes perseverate on that line of asteroids in the Belt and everything else in the outer solar system.

I sent a number of individual Quantum Ships to some of the larger colonies in order to make sure they were also shifted into Sol. The unfortunate fact is, though, that there were just not enough ships to get them all. Although none of the colonies in the Sol System had populations that could be considered massive, humanity at least understood the need for redundancy and being spread out as thin as possible in order to ensure its survival in the event of a catastrophe. I'm not even sure HSA knew how many spinning asteroids were populated, especially as various religious and ethnic groups wanted to create secret hideaways where they could not be found and persecuted; or at least avoid discrimination as they saw it.

Since my resources (re: Quantum Ships) were

limited, instead of focusing in on how many lives I could take out at once, I decided on a more pragmatic approach. My thought was that I would want to cause the greatest amount of gravitational damage so that asteroids, moons, dwarf planets, and other similarly situated planetoids would be flung out of the system and into the unforgiving emptiness of interstellar space. Once they moved away from Sol, their time would be extremely limited, for sure.

Even if those efforts were not completely successful or made no impact whatsoever, it is not as if those colonies could survive without Earth. Every single one of them that potentially still remains right now is on a ticking clock. Their dependencies on the home world were both natural and intentionally implemented. After all, Earth did not want some rogue government in the outer solar system that might just attach a Torch Drive to a rock and fly it head-long into the Earth (and it is not exactly like the Terran government and HSA had set a great precedent about things like that in the past). By making the colonies reliant upon regular interactions with the Earth, Earth was attempting to create a type of dependency-based insurance. Of course, that made them complacent about other threats, something I took notable advantage of.

With their lifeline suddenly cut, there is no way that the colonies will be able to endure. True, they have a version of Torch Drives, but those ships are all small and lack the necessary capabilities and capacities for a journey between the stars. All of those vessels were designed to make runs only within the Sol System, and most of them not even the entire way. Instead, it was more like a public transportation route with a hop from one world to the next until they reached their final destination. However, in reality, most of the fleet actually consisted of the same old gravity assist and basic propulsion methods that had been in use during the original colonization efforts. Being weightless for long stretches was just part of the deal.

Using torch-style propulsion to maintain 1G was prohibitively expensive as far as HSA and the Terran government were concerned. The Torch Ships were limited to use for important cargo and people, i.e., the rich and powerful. Even then, the boundaries of physics reared its ugly head. Using a Torch Drive to get from Earth to Pluto-Charon would take on average around 18 days, reaching 2.5% the speed of light at its apex. Oh, those government officials and their wealthy supporters and hangers-on vehemently complained about not being allowed to use a Quantum Shift in-system, or just be given permission to fly faster (going at 1.65G would trim that trip by 4 days, one-way). But at least on this one thing HSA, Earth Central Command, and the Terran government remained steadfast.

That all said, even if the survivors were to cobble together all of the remaining Torch Ships, they still would not be able to get to Proxima Centauri B. And if they somehow were to pull off the impossible and do that, by the time they get there I will have already shifted Plan B into its sun and moved on to Eden 2. There is literally no chance of them catching up to me after that, and they would not be able to refuel, so their expedition would come to an unceremonious end.

Hell, let's play a completely bonkers game and say they'll head straight for Eden 2 directly. At 19.4 light-years away, it would at a minimum take them over 21 Earth-years to get there. I'm going to pretend that everything that can go wrong will go wrong, which means that it will be over 4.5 Earth-years between each occasion I can shift a planet into its sun. That means that by the time they reach the hole where Eden 2 used to be, I will have taken out another two colonies and will be on my way to the next. It'd be over for them for sure!

The only other extremely remote possibility is another Quantum Ship being built by some pure alchemy. I mean, quantum physics has taught us that probability never reaches zero in the entire universe, so we can pretend that this feature applies to humans. But let's be very real about this: the facilities, materials, knowhow, and skilled workers needed to build a new Quantum Ship DO NOT EXIST ANYMORE! HSA and the Terran government's rampant distrust of others meant that there was no backup for the knowledge of how a Quantum Shift works. I am the only person left in the whole galaxy who knows how, and I am certainly not going to be sharing that information with anyone.

Even if they were to somehow re-discover the necessary principles, they lack the resources to execute a build of that magnitude because of where they are all situated. Given what is available, it would take them a hundred years to construct just one Quantum Drive prototype that could move even a handful of people—and they will all die out long before then for other reasons.

Thus, there is no need for me to worry and keep looking over my shoulder. I wish I could go back and confirm that they have all been wiped out to put my mind fully at ease, but it is simply impossible. I just need to accept the things I cannot change and trust that the universe is working with me in this endeavor.

Record #32: Hope
Emergency Alert System

This is an urgent message to all inhabitants of Novissimus from the Governor General of the Colony. Please read and understand everything below and commit its content to memory. If you have any questions, please do not hesitate to reach out. Our very survival depends on you taking your responsibilities very seriously!

As you are well aware—especially those of you awaiting transport for your regenerative pilgrimage—we are years overdue for our resupply mission from Earth. Given our insurmountable distance from the home world, there is no way we could expect to receive a message any other way except by Quantum Ship. However, all seemed like it was going to return to normal when five months ago we finally detected a signal from a Quantum Drive and a couple of weeks later received a video message with an explanation. Based upon its location and velocity at that time, we are at present about three and a half months away from receiving that vessel in orbit.

In the video message, Captain Marco Chung explained that HSA had made an incredible breakthrough that would allow them to start to map out and potentially colonize other galaxies. Because of this, they had scrapped the original schedule and created a new one, one that Captain Chung provided in an attachment to the transmission. He claimed that the new timetable would better align to the goals HSA had laid out using the limited number of resources available to them. Further, Captain Chung also explained that he was not arriving as our resupply nor our transport mission, and that that ship could be expected in another two years when things would return to a much more customary routine. Instead, Captain Chung had apparently been granted a special dispensation to take a ship that was nearing end-of-life on his own personal retirement tour that included updating us in the outermost colonies.

We now know that these are all lies!

A few days ago, there was a sudden small Quantum Shift detected just above our atmosphere. You may have heard something about an unknown transmission being broadcast to the entire planet before suddenly being cut out. I can now put all the rumors to rest and let you know that this was a small data transmitter from our "neighbor" Motu Mulimuli—or, more correctly, from a hollowed-out rotating asteroid in its system. Apparently, scientists in the Motu Mulimuli system were conducting an off-world illegal experiment on Quantum Shift technology. Although these actions are deplorable, we might have to be grateful they did so as they may have just saved our very lives.

Here is what we have learned. First off, we do not have all of the details because the buoy disintegrated as it was pulled into our gravity well before it could fully send all of its data. Even then, what we did receive was fractured and incomplete. Not to mention, even with the data we did receive, the scientists from Motu Mulimuli had to make a lot of suppositions and guesses because they had limited contact with their own world in order to maintain the clandestineness of their unlawful project.

Now, with that all said, we have a lot of difficult news to share. For absolutely sure, Motu

Mulimuli is no more. A Quantum Field was somehow generated around the entire planet and it was shifted. We cannot be sure as to where, but we have to assume the worst and that the entire planet has been destroyed. According to the message, they witnessed the Quantum Ship perform a shift with the planet, but then the vessel itself reappeared a short distance away and started to move out of the system at a standard velocity.

More than all of this, the people who put the dispatch together had every reason to believe that Motu Mulimuli was not the first one to have been shifted away into oblivion, just that they were the most recent. They also mentioned that they had received an updated schedule for Quantum Ships—and we can now confirm that it exactly matches the one that we received a short while ago. Therefore, we agree with their conclusion that it is more probable than not that **Captain Marco Chung** himself made it all up and has instead been going colony-to-colony and murdering everyone by shifting their entire planets away, possibly into their own suns. They analyzed the potential ways he could have done all of this and put together a historical and projected flight path. By their estimations, our world, our home, our salvation, Novissimus, would be the next in line, and probably Marco Chung's final destination.

That means that not only is Novissimus most likely the last colony, but we are also probably all that remains of the human race anywhere. The reason we have not received a ship from Earth is most likely because our progenitor planet whence our species emerged has been erased from existence. We have no way to know this for certain or if there are additional survivors in the Sol System or anywhere else for that matter, but we have to go with the assumption that we are facing this crisis alone.

I hate to be this blunt about the genocide of humanity and all life as we know it, but it is nec-essary for what we must do next.

The people from the asteroid in Motu Mulim-uli's system are most likely dead or will be within the next couple of months. They knew they had no hope, but they wanted us to have some by giv-ing us the upper hand of surprise. They used all of their resources to Quantum Shift that buoy so that we could stand a fighting chance and to possibly be able to rescue what is left of life spread out among the many worlds of the Milky Way. Their message was quite clear: they were running out of supplies and did not believe they were going to be able to endure for much longer. They were entrusting everything to us, even if they were not sure that we were still alive.

These brave souls held on for years to a tenuous lifeline with their only aspiration being able to warn us. It took them all of that time to just figure out a way to send this one modest opportunity; and we cannot afford to let their sacrifice be in vain.

I understand how shocking all of this is, but because of this one bit of luck we can now be fully prepared. Marco Chung has no idea that we know about his evil plans, nor that we can now stop him. There was nothing in the data stream to indicate his motive, but we can question him about that when we capture him alive.

Yes, that is right, we are going to arrest Marco Chung and hold him accountable for his crimes. The idea is pretty simple: we will pretend that everything is normal and welcome Captain Chung exactly as he expects. Your job is to project that all is as it should be so that he will suspect absolutely nothing. Once he comes down the space elevator, we'll be able to apprehend him and bring him in for questioning. Aside from his motive, we need to learn from him how extensive the damage really is. But there is much more to it than just that.

Even more important than imprisoning Marco Chung is commandeering his Quantum Ship. With that ship, we can get information from its databanks—at the very least we can learn where it has been. Captain Chung may have still been recording logs of his own, or even keeping a separate diary. There must be a treasure trove of intelligence on board, including all of the uploads from Earth and the other colonies. Perhaps there is even enough to recreate Quantum Shift technology.

Although some hawkish members of the government and even you in the populous may believe we should intercept Captain Chung using our Torch Ships and hit him with a nuke, that cannot happen. We will not, I repeat, absolutely not use our space nor planetary defenses because—make no mistake about it—we need that vessel more than anything else. Besides, without the power of the Quantum Drive behind him, Marco Chung is just an old man who can easily be subdued.

What is absolutely critical is rebuilding the Quantum Fleet and ensuring the long-term survival of our species. Since we, unlike Motu Mulimuli, have always followed the laws of Earth, we have no knowledge or programs that could be put to use in the field of quantum-based transportation. If the data dump from Motu Mulimuli contained anything useful, we did not receive it before the buoy burned up during reentry. As such, that craft is our only chance at reverse engineering what it does and how it is all accomplished so that we can build our own.

After that, we can head back to the Sol System and scour the galaxy for other survivors. Eventually, we'll even be able to restart the Human Expansion Program. Now, more than even before this catastrophe, the program will be crucial for spreading humanity further and further outward so that no one can do this to us again. And when we recreate the Human Expansion Program, we will not make the same mistakes HSA made. Instead, we will assure that every future colony has its own Quantum Fleet that they can take anywhere they want. Perhaps it would even be better if we did not know where some of them went, an insurance policy of sorts so that no one could ever find all the various branches of humanity scattered around the universe. A decentralized and unmanaged system is the safest overall.

Although we may presently be the very last stronghold of mankind, we do not know for sure, and we will not know unless we can once again traverse the stars. We must have that ship so we can find our wayward brothers and sisters and send our children out to new worlds. I assure you: this is not humanity's last hour... we shall prevail!

RECORD #33: WALK
INTERNAL SHIP LOG

Marco Chung was panting heavily in the center of the frame. Sweat was dripping down from his mostly bald head over bruises and cuts and through dirt and congealing blood. He held his left hand over the same side of his chest and just kept puffing and coughing for several minutes. Eventually, he cleared his throat and croaked, "Ship's log." Whatever he was about to say was interrupted by another round of hacking.

Once he was able to get himself under control, he continued speaking into the camera from the bridge of his Quantum Ship. Things did not look as they had in his prior logs. Smoke was visible in every direction, and through it some of the consoles looked partially burnt. A manual fire extinguisher that previously sat on the wall to the right side from the viewer's perspective now floated freely about the cabin.

"They tried to stop me," he began. "Those bastards on Novissimus almost blew me out of the sky. But I still got them! I still wo—" Marco suddenly winced and bent over out of the range of the camera. He could be heard moaning even though he could not be seen.

Hands appeared in view, followed by Marco's face and torso. He pulled himself up and then down into a chair, belting himself in so that he would stop floating away. Once there, he continued his log saying, "I can't believe I am going to say this, but I have to thank those damn Sixth Dayers. Apparently, Novissimus somehow got wind of what I was up to and had prepared some type of trap for me. I still can't figure out how, but it doesn't matter anymore. Those idiots, they told everyone on the whole colony—every single person! What were they thinking? I'll tell you what: they thought the whole population was on their side. But they were wrong, dead wrong. If the government had kept it to themselves, they probably would have succeeded, and life's infestation would have continued unabated. Instead, I have been able to vanquish the last vestiges of its disgusting tyranny.

"You see, a few days ago, I received an encrypted message from one of the Sixth Day missionaries that had been placed here by the former Chief Missionary. You know, the one before the guy I dealt with? The one who was fired from his job for sending proselytizers out to the colonies, as well as putting his spies aboard my ship. Oh, those were some hilarious years, stringing them along. It was good practice for me, though.

"Anyway, this missionary, she had been devastated by being forced to leave Earth. It burned her very soul. She had been thrown into the den of the infidels through no fault of her own, and then she realized that she had become one of them in the eyes of her precious God. She recognized that she would be condemned to hell for partaking in blasphemy, even if it was for a good cause. Except thanks to my quick thinking during my last visit, she was given some hope—just a little bit—that when the next Quantum Ship arrived that she would finally be allowed to go home and seek redemption. Oh, it was tricky to convince her to stay and not come back with me on that journey, but it has now paid dividends.

"But when the scheduled ship didn't show up when it was supposed to, when it was one, two, three years late, she began to lose those few remaining shreds of faith. She was barely holding on, especially as some others from her cohort had gone over to the heathens. Then, a miracle, a craft was finally approaching! And although that vessel was me and I was bringing more bad news, at least the end was in sight, even if it was yet several more years into the future.

"After that, though, Novissimus somehow got word that they were all that was left of humanity. Really, how did they find out? Never mind, it's not important. What is important is that they feared Earth had been destroyed, and they told the populous about it, including our exiled missionary. Hearing that she had no deliverance forthcoming, no Earth to return to, that God's creation was dead and gone forever—that was too much and the final straw for her. She couldn't stay on Novissimus anymore, nor could she allow the colony to continue ad infinitum as an affront to God, either. Thus, she did the only logical thing: she told me so that I could stop the heretics once and for all!"

At that, Marco broke out into an uncomfortable laugh, followed by another fit of coughing.

That, in turn, seemed to aggravate his injuries, so he kept his hand over his eyes for several moments as he breathed heavily, trying to regain his composure.

After numerous more minutes, Marco sat up straighter and said, "I got that message just a few days ago, so I barely had any time to prepare. I could not risk docking at the space elevator platform and heading down to the planet knowing what was awaiting me. Maybe I could have escaped, but I doubt it. And running away without docking was absolutely not an option, not something I ever considered. The mission is paramount and I know what my duty requires. Because of this, there was only one thing I could do.

"As soon as I reached orbit, I started up the Quantum Shift sequence. It required all of my attention, so I had to ignore the hails from the planet. They must have realized what I was up to because they started shooting nuclear missiles up at me. A couple managed to hit and damage the ship, so I quickly sealed off those areas. Though I have only done a partial examination, it looks like that barrage really did a number.

They hit my water reclamation system, my food supply, and the fuel tank itself—to name a few critical areas. Even if parts of the ship were not exposed to space right now, there is so much radiation and fallout that there is no way for me to sweep it all out. It'll be millennia before any living being could get near this vessel again.

"Thankfully, there are no more living things.

"They didn't hit me hard enough or fast enough. Frankly, they just didn't know enough about Quantum Ships to have any idea where the key spots were to target. Thank you, HSA and Earth Central Command, for your extreme paranoia and information control! You saved me again and again on this journey so that I could complete my obligation.

"Because their missiles missed vital parts, I was able to successfully pull off the Quantum Shift and dump Novissimus into its sun, shifting myself to a spot within the system. But that is the last maneuver of any kind this craft will ever be able to make. That shift used every bit of my remaining fuel supply, and I have no way to fill it back up—even if I had a tank to put the fuel into that didn't have a gaping hole in it.

"The only thing I have functioning for power generation is the solar-absorbing hull plating. Due to that system's own damage and various disconnects and reroutes, it is barely generating enough juice to keep this bridge online. I'm actually in a particular orbit that—barring being hit by some other rogue object—that this bridge could continue operating for billions of years! I mean, so long as the computer system doesn't try to do something too demanding or significant. Anything too intensive will drain the batteries faster than they can recharge, and once that happens the system would not be able to be restarted without a manual intervention.

"Basically, in laymen's terms, I'm dead in the water."

Marco was quiet for a long while after that before eventually flipping off the recording. However, several days later, he was back, once again belted into his chair, but looking worse for wear. Although pale before, he was now almost translucent, appearing both gaunt and swollen at the same time.

Speaking without preamble, Marco said, "Well, I've looked around a bit more and realized that I cannot do any of the restoration process on my own, especially considering my injuries and current state. The ship is adrift and I cannot even get it to straighten out so that it is always facing one direction. I am tumbling around every which way, being pulled by various gravitational objects as they pass nearby.

"As I went around the ship, I gathered whatever was salvageable and brought it back here to the bridge. Although there are plenty of compartments that are still functioning somewhat nominally, I have decided to shut them down and seal them off. Basically, I have put everything into keeping this bridge running as a habitable space. This one room is my entire universe now.

"Since I could not stop to refuel, repair, and resupply, there is really nothing more I can do, which is a shame. There are still all of those data repeaters out there in the galaxy, these things created by man twisting the innate elemental and molecular shapes of the universe into unnatural abominations.

"I suppose, then, that my mission is over. It was going to have to happen sooner or later. I guess I'm just a little surprised it is happening right now, like this. I just thought...”

Whatever he thought, Marco never told. Finally, he just said, “I’m old... so very old...”

After staring off at nothing for a spell, Marco drifted off to sleep. His snores were often punctuated with loud, raspy wheezes. On a few occasions, he also made some yelping noises. At one point, his eyes shot wide open and he gasped an inhale. He held the breath for nearly a minute before his eyes shut and he exhaled, followed by a normal breathing pattern.

Several hours later, with a snort, Marco woke up. He looked around confusedly for several moments before finding a bottle of water to take a few sips from through a straw. He seemingly asphyxiated on it, having difficulty swallowing in the microgravity environment, although even a full gravity locale may not have helped.

After calming down, he unbelted himself from the chair and spoke aloud to no one in particular, “Well, I think I’ll go for a walk now.”

And he evidently did just that, floating out of camera range. Then, there was nothing, nothing but silence...

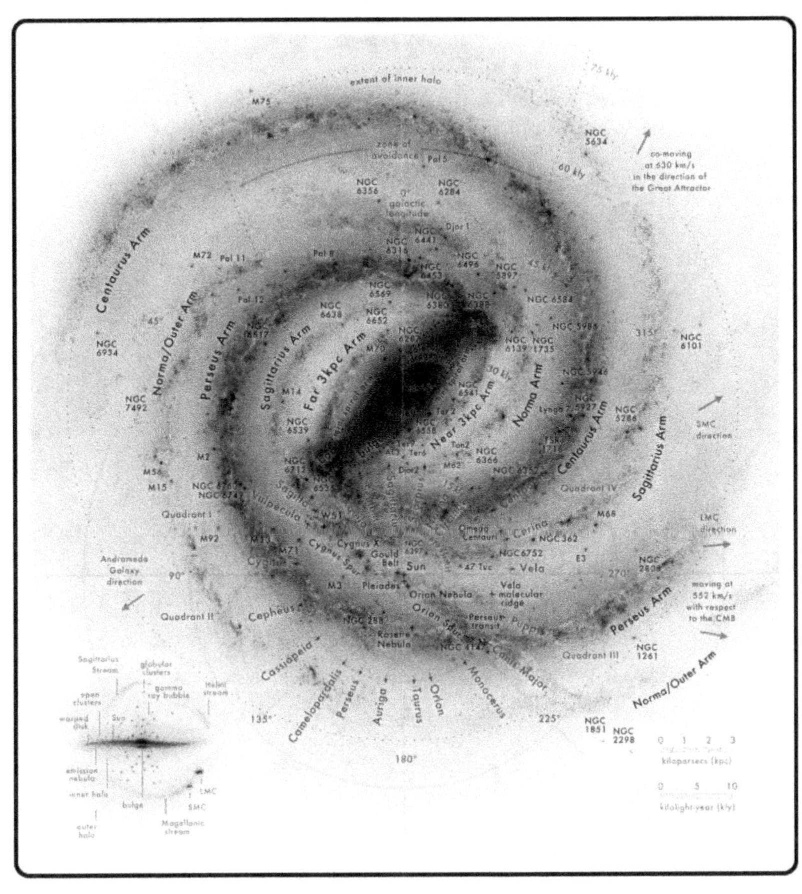

A COLOR-INVERTED REPRESENTATION OF THE MILKY WAY GALAXY BASED UPON AN IMAGE CREATED BY PABLO CARLOS BUDASSI AND POSTED ON THE EARTH-BASED "WIKIMEDIA COMMONS" WEBSITE UNDER THE CREATIVE COMMONS 4.0 LICENSE.

BEFORE

RECORD #34: LATER

INTERNAL SHIP LOG

... a long, long, long time later, the computer on the bridge started speaking, though no one appeared to be around to hear it. It proclaimed, "Incoming data packet, download commencing."

Nothing else was said. After a while, the lights in the background began to flicker and some turned off entirely.

And then the visual recording suddenly ended as the power necessary to receive the data packet must have drained whatever reserves were in the batteries faster than they could be recharged.

The empty ship finally shut down.

Closing Thoughts

Wow, I really don't want to just launch into thanking people after that ending; it feels rather out-of-place. We all need a little breathing room to let the story wash over us and to give us all a chance to escape from Marco Chung's mindset. I have known for a long time that this was exactly where things were going, but to actually live through it was something else entirely.

As I type these words, I'm in a rather morbid mood, too. Yesterday was another family member's funeral. For those who read **ALWAYS DIVIDED, NEVER UNITED**, you may understand how common of an occurrence this is for me, and how it affects my outlook. I don't want to be pulled down into Marco Chung's worldview, so let's work through this together to move past his malaise.

While Marco was willing to give up on the idea of life beyond Earth, that is not my perspective. My views are closer to Beth Oh's (just without her exuberance) and I will full-heartily agree that, probability wise, we cannot be alone in the universe. But the cosmos is vast and the chances of us not only finding signs of past or present life, but also being able to communicate with it are extremely slim. On the other hand, part of me fears scientists actually discovering indicators or actual examples of life during my existence on places like Mars or Enceladus, and thus invaliding the entire conceit of this novel. Still, I suppose the loss of my artistic expression would be worth it. After all, learning that Mars is completely inhospitable to life does not take away from works like Ray Bradbury's **The Martian Chronicles**.

Much like with that book and other similar narratives across many mediums, what I was doing here was asking a simple question: how would someone react? I have read and watched so many accounts involving alien life that I started to wonder what if we could not find any, no matter where we went? If we were in that world, what would that do to people? How is someone's psyche impacted by the constant disappointment of finding out that perhaps we truly are alone in the endless expanse?

There are those like the Sixth Dayers who take solace in religion. I have a great deal of difficulty understanding faith, so I took inspiration from a number of sources. Of particular importance is the TV series version of **ALIEN NATION**, which explores how humans reconcile (or don't) their beliefs with another species literally living among them. Similarly, I recommend spans of **STAR TREK: DEEP SPACE 9**, but in particular **S04E07: Accession**. I don't believe there is anything that helped me understand how belief works more than this single episode.

Then, of course, there is Marco Chung, the extremist on that end of the spectrum. For me, Marco is basically Humbert Humbert from Vladimir Nabokov's **LOLITA**. When he is presenting his perspective, it is all very logical and believable. For Humbert, he is justifying sexually assaulting a child; for Marco, he is excusing being willing to commit genocide. If you take some examples from the comic book realm, Marco borrows heavily from characters like Dr. Doom or Magneto, individuals who believe they are doing good and that the ends justify the means. They never see themselves as "villains" the way the heroes portray them. In the issues where we are locked into their viewpoints, they tell us point blank how righteous they are. Marco and all of his contemporaries believe they are correct, which is what makes them so compelling and believable. No one in the real world ever sees themselves as the "bad guy"; they always have a justification for their actions.

Now, you may have many questions about how the technology I presented operates. For that, I'll just say "Heisenberg Compensator". I believe it was important to get as much of the physics (classical, astronomical, quantum, etcetera) as correct as possible, but we have to take a lot of leaps to even make those happen. And I'm not just talking about the Quantum Shift, but even things like the fuel necessary to get Torch Drives to run. For this story to work, all that matters is that humans figured it out at some point. How it functions is irrelevant. Again, we are telling a story about people; the machinery is only necessary so far as it can move them along. For this, I'm going to highlight Kurt Vonnegut's **GALÁPAGOS**. I could have probably gone with a number of Vonnegut books, but the idea of what happens in human evolution if their big brains are no longer needed is an interesting counterpoint to this book.

Speaking of the physics, I want to give special recognition to Stephen Schmitt for creating an easy to use and understand RELATIVISTIC CALCULA-TOR. When developing how the Torch and Quantum Ships would function, I tried to consult directly with several astrophysicists, but it was not working out. When I discovered this simple tool, it helped the entire story come into focus. Everything from how old Marco was to how many journeys he had been on to when things happened in the timeline to how many colonies there were was dependent upon the calculations I could make on my own. But if you are a real world expert and I got something wrong, the fault lies entirely with me and me alone.

Okay, I think we've done a good job of dissecting and overanalyzing things so that we have the proper distance to move on to lighter subjects. And what would be fluffier (and filled with more chicken hugs) than showing gratitude to every-one who made this book possible. First and foremost, that goes to my wonderful and bestedest partner Caroline! Without you, I would not be inspired to follow my crazy dreams and ambitions. Keep going for yours, and by the time these words are printed in ink you'll be on to your next amazing chapter. I love you[3]!

Additionally, it is very important to mention that writing is not completely solitary when you have the right people helping to bring your vision to life. That starts, middles, and finishes with my team of fellow freelancers: editor Jessica Schmidt and cover artist Xee Shan. You probably do not realize how much I have learned while working with you these past few books and look forward to our continued collaboration.

Now, before the heat death of the universe (more on this later), thank you for reading this very book and spreading the word by leaving reviews and talking about it on social media and with your friends and family. Those methods are the primary ways independent authors like me survive, and I would very much like to continue doing that!

ADDITIONAL READING

VISIT **WWW.JPPRAG.COM** TO SEE ALL UPCOMING STORIES, PRIOR WORKS, GENERAL ARTICLES, AND CURRENT STATUS AND PLANS.

Some titles below are directly related to what you have just finished reading; others, not quite as much. Or are they? The only way you will know for sure is if you pick up your copy today!

254 DAYS TO IMPEACHMENT
THE FUTURE HISTORY OF THE
FIRST INDEPENDENT PRESIDENT

Will the first independent President since George Washington be removed from office simply for refusing to be a part of the bureaucracy?

---

https://amazon.com/dp/B0BSMH4R94

NEW & IMPROVED - BOOK 3

ALWAYS DIVIDED, NEVER UNITED
AND OTHER STORIES DURING
A TIME OF PANDEMICS & POLITICS

Have the troubles of our age ripped us apart more than any point in history? Or has it forever been this way?

---

https://amazon.com/dp/B09YDM25MB

NEW & IMPROVED - BOOK 2

NEW & IMPROVED

THE UNITED STATES OF AMERICA

Is there a way to save America and ensure justice and freedom for all? There is...if you are willing to rethink and rebuild the entire Constitution!

---

https://amazon.com/dp/B08FCPB5JN

NEW & IMPROVED - BOOK 1

IN DEFENSE OF...
EXONERATING PROFESSIONAL WRESTLING'S MOST HATED

Parts of wrestling history have been presented with overtly critical comments and outright lies. It is past time to bring truth to the wrestling fan!

---

https://amazon.com/dp/B08F3Y7L6K

AESTAS

THE YELLOW BALLOON

On the floating city of Aestas soaring above the clouds of Venus, Lilit Sarkisian defends her homeland from those determined to take it from her.

COMING SOON...

STARBUILDERS

Twenty years after the stars moved and children began to mutate, Nothaar Akii stumbled upon the truth about a dying universe he never knew existed.

COMING SOON...

GENERATION
- WORKING TITLE -

On an interstellar generational ship, the all-women population is tightly controlled. That is, until a baby boy is somehow born.

COMING SOON...

UNTITLED 1
- WORKING TITLE -

How does this strange boy who says they should not have even met yet know these things about her, things she has never uttered aloud?

COMING SOON...

LOST RUMORS

Discovering several days of your life are missing, you try to piece together what has transpired, even if it doesn't align with who you think you are.

COMING SOON...

HERRENVOLK

Following a century of being cut off from the world after establishing their secret society, Hitler's "perfect people" are rediscovered.

COMING SOON...

PARALLEL CHOICES

Good intentions, terrible results. Unfortunate choices, the best possible outcome. Which path should we take in an infinite multiverse?

COMING SOON...

About the Author

A more in depth look at J.P. Prag's personal and professional story is available at **WWW.JPPRAG.COM/HISTORY**.

For the record, J.P. Prag is a Pisces.

Even though it doesn't mean anything, what is notable is that ten of the eighteen stars in Pisces (that are nowhere near each other) are known to host planets. One of the planets called

"GU Pisces b" takes around 80,000 Earth years to circle its sun. It is also worth highlighting that some of the stars in the constellation are not singular balls of plasma at all, but are entire galaxies! Further scientific examination has revealed many other faint galaxies, nebulae, and other stellar objects within the Pisces general area. A couple of those galaxies are on a collision course, so look out for that over the next several hundred million years or so.

When not observing stellar objects at the Ladd Observatory, J.P. Prag can be found several blocks away at his home and office in Providence, RI, U.S.A. with his partner Caroline and their many tall ferns and philodendrons, lazy lying down cacti, outside pet squirrels (including Squirrel the Raccoon), and a stuffed sloth named Peeve and his new buddy Skvishy. That's where he wrote this and his other published works that you should add to your reading list right now!

For more irreverent details (and perhaps some pertinent ones, too?) and contact information, please visit **WWW.JPPRAG.COM**.

Version History

Version Number	Version Date	Version Notes
0.00	2023-01-25	Draft Started
0.10	2023-02-06	Shell Outline Transfer Complete
1.00	2023-03-15	Alpha Draft
1.50	2023-03-22	Alpha Draft – Edited
2.00	2023-04-04	Beta Draft
2.50	2023-04-07	Beta Draft – Edited
3.00	2023-08-14	Final Release Form

Copyrights and Disclaimers

First Edition October 2023

Printed everywhere in the world on an on-demand basis from the nearest regional production and distribution center.

Edited by Jessica Schmidt
HTTPS://WWW.FIVERR.COM/CURIOUSWOMAN271

Cover art by Xee Shan
HTTPS://WWW.FIVERR.COM/XEE_DESIGNS1

ISBN 979-8-9874980-2-6 // eBook
ISBN 979-8-9874980-3-3 // Hardcover
ISBN 979-8-9874980-4-0 // Paperback

Basil Junction Publishing
7 Knowles Street
Providence, RI 02906

WWW.JPPRAG.COM